W9-CCP-117

DR. DOLITTLE

OTHER YEARLING BOOKS YOU WILL ENJOY:

YEARLING BOOKS are designed especially to entertain and enlighten young people. Patricia Reilly Giff, consultant to this series, received her bachelor's degree from Marymount College and a master's degree in history from St. John's University. She holds a Professional Diploma in Reading and a Doctorate of Humane Letters from Hofstra University. She was a teacher and reading consultant for many years, and is the author of numerous books for young readers.

DR. DOLITTLE

BASED ON THE SCREENPLAY BY

Nat Mauldin and Larry Levin

**BASED ON THE CHARACTER CREATED BY
NEWBERY AWARD–WINNING AUTHOR HUGH LOFTING**

NOVELIZATION BY N. H. KLEINBAUM

A YEARLING BOOK

Published by
Bantam Doubleday Dell Books for Young Readers
a division of
Bantam Doubleday Dell Publishing Group, Inc.
1540 Broadway
New York, New York 10036

If you purchased this book without a cover you should be aware that this book is stolen property. It was reported as "unsold and destroyed" to the publisher and neither the author nor the publisher has received any payment for this "stripped book."

Text and photographs copyright © 1998 by
Twentieth Century Fox Film Corporation

Photographs courtesy of Phil Bray

All rights reserved. No part of this book may be reproduced or transmitted in any form or by any means, electronic or mechanical, including photocopying, recording, or by any information storage and retrieval system, without the written permission of the Publisher, except where permitted by law.

The trademarks Yearling® and Dell® are registered in the U.S. Patent and Trademark Office and in other countries.

Visit us on the Web!
www.bdd.com

Educators and librarians, visit the
BDD Teacher's Resource Center at
www.bdd.com/teachers

ISBN: 0-440-41546-2

Printed in the United States of America
July 1998
10 9 8 7 6 5 4
OPM

Prologue

Lucky was an old mutt. He sprawled on the asphalt in the alleyway, chomping on a chicken leg and watching his dog friends check out the trash cans for a snack.

"How'd you get the good stuff?" a black retriever yelled. Lucky took a big bite of the chicken leg and smiled.

"Just lucky, I guess." He laughed.

Spike the schnauzer jumped into a trash can and fell to the bottom. "Help!" he cried. His pals laughed and gathered around. One of the dogs tipped the can over, letting Spike escape.

"Thanks, guys," Spike said. They resumed their positions on the asphalt. "You done with that chicken yet?" Spike asked Lucky.

"Sure," Lucky said, tossing Spike the leftovers. Lucky lay back and looked up at the bright sun and the cloudless blue sky above the San Francisco skyline.

"Did I ever tell you guys the story about my incredible baseball catch?" he asked. Without waiting for a reply, he closed his eyes and said dreamily, "So the ball is going way, way back and I'm running. Last minute, I jump like ten feet straight up . . ." He opened his eyes and stood on all fours. "*Whomp!* I make this incredible catch!"

"Yeah, *right*," his pals teased. "Your stories are so lame," Spike said, guarding the piece of chicken.

"Okay, okay, I've got another story. You'll love it. And you know the best part of it?" Lucky asked.

"It's short?" Rocky the retriever asked.

"No." Lucky smiled as he got into a more comfortable position, ready to spin his tale. "It's *true*. This is a story about me, the tiger, and the incredible Dr. Dolittle."

"You know Dr. Dolittle?" Spike asked in awe.

"Name-dropper," Rocky snorted. "You're such a liar."

Lucky paused and looked seriously around at his audience of dog friends.

"May I get worms if this isn't true," he said.

Suddenly they were all silent, staring at Lucky. In the dog world getting worms was about as serious as it could get.

"Sit," he said to the crowd as they moved closer. "I mean, have a seat. I gotta start at the very beginning. It all began in Eureka, California, in 1962. . . ."

John Dolittle rolled around on the grass in the front yard of his house, playing with his dog. The five-year-old African American boy sat in front of the animal, barking as the dog barked back. Above them a squirrel scampered out on a tree branch, and a sparrow perched on a limb nearby. The squirrel and sparrow squawked and chatted, joining in on the barking conversation between John and his dog. John waved to them and they came down. John chatted with the animals, answering them in their languages.

Sitting on the porch of the house, John's father and mother watched their son with concern.

"It's not normal," Archer Dolittle said, shaking his head and frowning. "Not healthy." He watched as John stretched out his arms and dozens of birds

3

landed on his sleeves. They chirped happily and he chirped in answer, smiling.

Suddenly three teenage boys rode up on motorbikes, pointing at John and laughing.

"Hey, hey!" Archer yelled. The kids scattered at the sight of the tall man running down the steps. "Come back here, you little cowards, so I can bang your empty heads together!" he shouted.

The dog barked and whisked past Archer, chasing the fleeing bikers. John followed his dog, barking too.

Archer sighed and walked back onto the porch. "We've got to do something," he said to his wife. "The boy's got no friends. He's talking to the animals all the time." He shook his head. "I've decided. I'm taking that job in Oakland and that's final. We've got to get out of here."

"Archer, they've got animals in Oakland, too," his wife said softly. "We can't run away from this."

"We've got to try something!" her husband almost shouted. "He needs a fresh start. I already spoke to Jim and Nancy. There's a nice apartment opening up right above them. Lots of kids running around—he's gonna be happy. He'll have friends who are kids—not animals."

"They don't allow pets in that building, Archer," Mrs. Dolittle said.

4

Her husband sat in silence.

"You can't take that dog away from him!" she exclaimed.

Her husband sat rigid. "He needs a fresh start. He needs *people* friends."

John raced back up the street with the dog, breathless but smiling. "Lucy got rid of those bullies," he laughed. "Stupid kids." His parents looked at him silently.

"Hey, what's up, what happened? Somebody die or something?" John asked.

"No, honey, of course not." His mother smiled and waved him up onto the porch. "Nothing bad. Actually it's really good news."

"What good news?" John asked suspiciously, looking at his father's grave expression.

"Daddy got a new job! Isn't that exciting?" his mother said. "And we're going to be moving to Oakland. To a beautiful apartment near Jim and Nancy and their kids. There's a great school and lots of kids."

John was shocked. "Moving? To an apartment? Without a yard and grass and trees and places to run? What's Lucy gonna do in an apartment all day? This is terrible!" he wailed.

His mother smiled, trying to cheer him up. "Well, that's the thing. We can't have a pet like Lucy in the apartment. But Jimmy Jones's mom said they'd take

5

good care of her, and you can visit her whenever you like."

"And we could get a smaller, indoor pet," his father said. "Wouldn't that be great?"

John glared at his parents. "Great? It stinks! I don't want to move and I don't want to live in an apartment and I don't want Jimmy Jones to get Lucy! And I *don't* want another pet!" He opened the screen door, ran into the house, and slammed it behind him. Lucy sat whimpering on the porch, looking hard at John's parents.

"Oh, dear," Mrs. Dolittle sighed.

"He'll get used to it, just you wait," Archer said. "It's for the best."

He looked at Lucy, whining on the porch, then got up and opened the door. "Maybe *you* can calm him down," he said to the dog. Lucy scampered inside the house.

Several weeks later a moving van pulled up in front of the Dolittles' house and a team of workers began loading it. Men carried out boxes, furniture, lamps, and bookcases. The family car was packed up and John's neighbor Jimmy Jones held Lucy by a leash on the lawn. John stood on the front porch. Tears streamed down his face as his parents tried to comfort him.

"I'm sorry we can't take Lucy, son. Doggies don't like the city much—she'll be so much happier out here," his father said. John wiped his tears away and headed toward the car. The squirrel zipped out on his tree limb, the sparrow landed on the fence, and a couple of other neighborhood dogs ran up and down the sidewalk, happy to see John and unaware of what was happening. They barked and squawked at John as he neared the car, but John just walked past them silently, ignoring every animal.

The animals kept calling out to him.

Suddenly John grabbed a rock, spun around, and angrily threw it as hard as he could. The animals were stunned into silence. They stared at John as he climbed into the front seat of the car, slamming the door. His parents watched from the porch as they locked the house door for the last time.

"He's going to be just fine," Archer said to his wife. "Let's go." As they walked to the car he turned to the line of animals. "Scat!" he shouted. "Get outta here!"

The family sat in the front seat. Mr. Dolittle drove away to the sound of Lucy barking in the distance.

The Dolittle family settled happily in Oakland, and John adjusted to his new life in spite of his initial objections. He made friends and was popular with his classmates, enjoyed sports, and was considered an all-around good guy. He studied hard in school and, much to his parents' delight, was an excellent student.

He grew up, went to UCLA, met a young woman named Lisa, and was swept off his feet. When they'd graduated they got married. She worked as a schoolteacher while he attended medical school. After his medical training, Dr. John Dolittle opened his own practice in San Francisco, treating sick people. He was outgoing and friendly, and his patients loved him. Soon the practice grew, as did his family. Lisa stopped teaching when their daughter Charisse was born, later followed by Maya. The family lived in a large, comfortable apartment overlooking the Golden Gate Bridge and the hills of Sausalito.

Dr. John Dolittle joined two friends from medical school to form a group practice, and the practice flourished. By 1997 they were being sought by the biggest medical company in the state, Calnet, which wanted to buy their prestigious practice for an enormous sum of money.

One night the Dolittle family sat on the king-sized bed in John and Lisa's room watching the movie *Sounder* on their big-screen TV. The dramatic tale of an old dog and a family of sharecroppers moved the girls and Lisa to tears. Nickel-sized teardrops slid down Charisse's beautiful teenage face. Nine-year-old Maya grabbed the tissue box and blew her nose loudly, passing the box to her mother, who sobbed outright. Lisa passed the tissue box to John, who absentmindedly set it down as he studied a thick folder containing Calnet's business proposal.

"Daddy," Maya cried when the movie went to a commercial. "You're not watching! How could you not watch?"

"I am. I am," he said without looking up. "Flounder's barking, Daddy's home, and everyone's happy."

"It's *Sounder,* Dad," Charisse said, and snickered.

Dolittle continued to turn the pages of the report. "Of course it is."

Lisa blew her nose and shook her head. "I can't believe I married a man who doesn't cry at *Sounder.*" She blew her nose again and shook her head.

John looked up at his sniffling relatives. "Somebody has to stay strong in this family," he said. "What if there was an earthquake during this movie? All of you would be misty-eyed, bumping into things, tripping and falling all over each other . . ."

"Oh, Daddy!" Maya said.

Lisa shook her head. "Just go back to work," she sighed as the commercial ended and the movie resumed.

The next morning Maya jumped out of bed and raced to her desk. A large egg sat under a lamp. She picked it up carefully, walking past a room filled with science equipment and experiments in progress and went to the kitchen.

"Look how big my egg is getting, Daddy," she said when her father entered the room.

"Super," he smiled, tying his tie and checking his beeper. "Morning, Charisse," he said to his older daughter, who sat morosely at the table.

"I'm not Charisse anymore. I've changed my name to Paprika," Charisse answered.

"Hmmm." Her father nodded. "Paprika Dolittle. Has a lovely ring to it."

"Not Dolittle," she corrected. "Just Paprika."

John turned toward Lisa, who was cooking breakfast. "Honey, did you hear that? She's not a Dolittle anymore. She's just . . . *Paprika*."

"I've been informed." Lisa chuckled.

Maya came to her sister's defense. "I think Paprika's a beautiful name," she said.

"I think it's a seasoning," her father said, reaching for the telephone. "Hello . . . Mark. Yeah, I've been going over the proposal. Unbelievable . . ."

Maya shook her head. "He doesn't take anything we want seriously anymore," she complained.

"Tell me about it," Charisse agreed.

Still on the telephone, Dolittle said, "Yeah, if these guys are for real, then I'm very interested. I'll be in the office soon." He hung up the phone.

Maya got up from the table and tried to sneak an empty egg carton off the counter.

"Where are you going with that?" her mother asked.

"It's for my swan egg. I found it in the park," Maya explained, holding up the oversized egg.

"Looks like it would make a nice omelet," her father said with a laugh.

"*Dad!* It's gonna hatch any day now."

"But honey," Lisa said, "you're going to be in camp!"

Maya shook her head. "Mom, I've decided I can't go to camp. I have to be here when it hatches 'cause a baby bird bonds with the first thing it sees and I want that to be me."

Dolittle looked at his daughter with a stern expression. "Maya, it is not normal or healthy to stay in your room all the time with your little experiments. You want to do an experiment? Try spending time with kids your age. *At camp,*" he said. He gathered his things to go. "Which is exactly where we're dropping you off Sunday on our way back from the country."

"You mean *dumping* me off," Maya said. "And what about my pet egg?"

Her father handed her a half-filled egg carton. "Here's a half a dozen pets. You can take all of them to camp with you," he said.

"Daddy!" Maya protested.

"John!" Lisa echoed. "There's nothing wrong with girls being interested in science and pets." Turning to Maya, she added, "But honey, you can't take an egg, even one, to camp. It's just not allowed. I'll watch your egg, and I'm sure it won't hatch before you get home."

"But that's four weeks!" Maya wailed. "It looks like it will pop before that, doesn't it, Daddy?"

Dr. Dolittle took the egg from her and pretended

to examine it. "Ms. Dolittle," he said, "I'm sure you won't become a mother to this egg for at least four weeks. Besides, didn't we buy you a pet? That—that—what was it?"

"Guinea pig!" Maya said.

"*Right*. I can't help it if it died." Her father shrugged.

The rest of the Dolittles looked at each other in confusion. "It didn't die!" Maya shouted. "His name is Rodney and he's in my room."

John Dolittle waved his arms. "Oh, well, that's great, isn't it? Then everything's okay, right?" He picked up his folders, checked his beeper, and kissed his wife goodbye. "Gotta go. Work time. I love you all." He looked at his older daughter. "Bye, Oregano!"

"It's *Paprika*!" Charisse said, rolling her eyes.

Her father slipped out of the kitchen with a smile as his wife followed him to the hall.

"John, you're starting to sound just like your father!" she said, shaking her head.

He kissed her on the nose. "Love you. Bye!" he said, and went out the door. He took the elevator down to the parking level and opened the door of his red car. He started up the motor and whizzed out of the lot onto the rolling streets of San Francisco. He stopped in front of an imposing four-story brick medical complex, swung left into the parking lot, and pulled into a spot marked DR. DOLITTLE.

He took the elevator to the fourth floor, got off, and stood for a moment in front of a door with gold lettering: DR. JOHN DOLITTLE, DR. GENE REISS, DR. MARK WELLER.

"Not bad," he said happily to himself as he opened the door to a huge wood-paneled waiting room already filled with patients sitting on an assortment of leather chairs and sofas. "Good morning, all," he said cheerily, cutting through a side door to the back office. He paused for a moment and listened to Diane, the receptionist, juggling telephone calls: "Doctor's office, hold, please. Doctor's office, hold, please. You were interested in an appointment *when?*"

Dolittle headed into his office, put his jacket on a hanger, and slipped into a white coat. He picked up a pile of patients' folders and started reviewing them.

Outside his office, Dr. Mark Weller, an ambitious, driven man, and Dr. Gene Reiss, a more indecisive man but an excellent doctor, walked down the hall, talking.

"It's a beautiful proposal, Gene," Weller said. "Incredible! Like a dream come true."

"Maybe, Mark, but I have qualms. Sometimes if something seems too good it's not as good as it looks," Reiss said.

"Look, at least talk to John about it," Weller suggested, knocking on Dolittle's door.

"Come in," Dolittle called. The three doctors talked for a minute about selling their company to Calnet, the big medical company that had offered them an enormous amount of money. Weller and Dolittle wanted to sell, but Reiss wasn't sure they should. Reiss liked the office the way it was.

"We'll discuss it on Monday," Dolittle said. "I'm going away with my family for the weekend."

"You can't, Dolittle. We have to meet these Calnet guys for breakfast Saturday. You have to be there."

"I'm supposed to take my family to the country on Friday," Dolittle protested.

"Well, now you can't," Weller said. "We have to have this meeting."

"*See*," Reiss said, "it's already happening—you're being forced to neglect your family because of Calnet."

Go to the country with his family or meet with Calnet—Dolittle wasn't sure what to do.

That night the Dolittle family prepared to pack up for the trip to the country. Lisa was angry because Dolittle had come home and announced that he couldn't go because of the Calnet meeting.

"I hope this deal is worth it," she said.

Dolittle laughed. "I'll be there right after the meeting Saturday. I promise. I won't even stop for red lights."

Lisa turned and glared. "John, Maya needs you. It's her last weekend before camp," she said. "She's more than a little nervous about going."

"She's gonna love it once she gets there," Dolittle told his wife.

Lisa shook her head. "I'm not so sure it's a good idea."

"Well, I am," her husband said.

Maya ran into the room in a panic. "Rodney is lost!" she cried. "We've got to find him."

Lisa sighed. "Not again."

"You guys gotta get going," Dolittle said. "I'll look for the hamster later."

"Daddy! He's a guinea pig!"

"Sorry, I get my rodents all mixed up," Dolittle laughed. He picked up several pieces of luggage and called for Charisse. "Come on, Nutmeg, let's get going!"

Charisse stuck her head out of her room. "Daddy! It's Paprika!"

"Right, right," he said. "I get those spices mixed up too."

Lisa pulled Maya aside and whispered as they left, "Don't worry, honey, your daddy will be sure to find him!" Maya smiled and skipped out the door.

Down in the parking lot, Lisa and the girls climbed into the van.

"Now Daddy, remember, you *have* to find Rodney," Maya reminded her father.

Dolittle nodded. "I'll tear the place upside down. I'll find him and bring him out for the weekend. Drive safe, now." He threw them a kiss. Lisa started up the van and headed out of the parking spot. Maya yelled from the car window, "Call me if my egg starts to hatch!"

Dolittle stood on the sidewalk and waved until the van was out of sight. Maybe a good night's sleep was just what he needed. That way, he thought, he'd be fresh for the meeting and still be able to meet his family in the country. He hurried back to the apartment to look for Rodney.

3

The next morning, after finding Maya's guinea pig in one of his shoes and putting him in his cage, Dolittle drove to the store to pick up a cup of coffee and the newspaper. On his way home, he put the coffee in the car's drink holder and rubbed his eyes. Suddenly he hit a bump in the road. The coffee spilled and he took his eyes off the road to grab a tissue and clean up the mess. When he looked back to the road, Dolittle was shocked to see a dog crossing in front of the car. He slammed on the brakes, swerved, and crashed into a mailbox, banging his head against the ceiling of the car. Shaken, he sat for several moments, put his head on the steering wheel, and closed his eyes to collect himself. He took a deep breath and looked into the road, where a mixed-breed dog lay. The dog was not moving.

Dolittle shook his head and sighed. "Oh, no!"

He sat and stared at the dog. He felt a lump rise in his throat. He shook his head, and tears came to his eyes. Dolittle grabbed a tissue and was wiping his eyes when suddenly he heard a voice:

"Watch where you're going next time, bonehead!"

Dolittle turned toward the voice. The dog that had been lying in the road was now walking across it. Dolittle leaped from the car. "Hey!" he called, but the dog ran off down the road.

Dolittle hit his head with his hand. "I need to get more sleep if I'm hearing dogs talk." He climbed back into the car, not noticing a squirrel, an owl, and a possum, in a tree above. They watched him drive away.

An hour later he was downtown with Mark Weller and Gene Reiss at an outdoor cafe. With them were Barton Calloway, head of Calnet, and his number two man, Jeremy Carson.

"I just wanted to thank you guys for giving up part of your weekend. This was the only time we had available," Calloway said.

"No problem." Weller smiled. "Thank *you*!"

"Anyway," Calloway continued, "we're here to answer any and all questions. We want you all to be comfortable with what we're proposing."

"Speaking of which," Carson said, handing each doctor a folder, "this explains the deal. The information you're probably most interested in is on page four."

The three doctors anxiously turned to page four and saw how much money Calnet would pay them.

Dolittle whistled. "That's a lot."

"We're very comfortable," Weller said. "Right, Gene?"

"Well," Reiss said, "I have some questions—"

"No you don't," Weller interrupted, cutting him off.

"Yes I do," Reiss said firmly.

"Oh, c'mon, fellas," Weller said, "let's not get wrapped up in little details, now."

As Dolittle looked over the contract, he heard a voice. "Bread?" someone asked him.

"No, thanks," Dolittle replied.

Weller looked at him. "No, thanks, for what?"

"I don't want any bread," Dolittle said, looking strangely at Weller. "You asked me if I wanted bread. I said no, thanks."

Calloway looked at the three doctors. "So you don't have a problem with the deal?" he asked.

"Bread," Dolittle heard again. He looked up. There was no bread on the table, nor was there a waiter with bread in sight. Dolittle turned and looked over the fence. There stood two squirrels gobbling up bread crumbs from the sidewalk. "More bread," he heard one of the squirrels say.

"Is this a joke or what?" Dolittle said, turning back to the table.

"Absolutely not!" Calloway said. He was talking about the deal.

The squirrel's voice said, "Hey, look! Spilled chips. Fritos!" The squirrels scurried after a man who was walking with a bag of chips in his arms and dropping some as he ate. Dolittle stared, confused as to who was talking. Calloway stared at Dolittle.

"So, do you have a problem or not, John?" Calloway asked.

Dolittle shook his head and snapped back to the meeting. "Uh, problem? No, no problem. It's just, it's really noisy out here, isn't it? All the voices are . . ."

The other men looked at him and shrugged. None of them were bothered by any noises or voices. Dolittle sat on the edge of his seat, keeping an ear out for strange sounds.

Reiss brought the talk back to the deal. "We'll have to read this carefully," he said. "Is it true that Calnet doesn't allow its doctors to tell patients about certain medicine if it costs too much?"

Dolittle looked at Calloway, trying to concentrate on his words. He suddenly heard the sound of someone gagging and turned around. He saw and heard one squirrel yelling at another one that was choking on something.

"That's too big a piece, you dimwit," the squirrel said. "I told you not to stuff yourself!"

Dolittle stared, ignoring the conversation at the table.

"John?" Calloway asked, interrupting Dolittle's observations. "Are you with us?"

"I'm sorry," Dolittle apologized to the men at table. "I had a tough night. Wife's out of town and we're not apart very often, so . . ."

"Hey, look, corn nuts over here," Dolittle heard the squirrel yell. Dolittle looked at the men around the table. Where were these voices coming from? "I'm a little scattered, but the deal's solid. I'm excited! Very, very, very excited," he told them. He jumped up from his seat. A bird flew past him. "Outta the way, pinhead," the bird told Dolittle. Dolittle looked at the men. No one else had heard the bird talk! Was he going nuts? He had to get home!

"Okay, so it's been a great meeting! Great meeting!" Dolittle told them. "But I've got to go. My family is up in the country. I'll—we'll all talk Monday, so have a great weekend. Bye!" Dolittle ran off before anyone could stop him.

Dolittle hurried to his car, jumped in, started the car, and drove home.

After a quick shower, he changed into casual clothes, picked up his small suitcase and Rodney's cage, and went back to the car. He put the guinea pig's cage on the seat next to him, relieved that he'd found the little rodent and could bring it to Maya. He drove out of the city, at once beginning to relax and enjoy the drive.

"The air is so fresh out here," a voice said.

"Yeah," Dolittle agreed. "That's the thing about the city. You don't realize—" He gave a look at Rodney in the cage and lost control of the car. He careened to the side of the road and smashed through several road signs before screeching to a halt.

"Jeez, Louise, that didn't seem too safe," Rodney said.

Dolittle checked the radio. It was off. He checked his cell phone. It was off too. He looked at the backseat. No one was there, only his small suitcase. He slowly looked down at the guinea pig. Could *this* be talking to *him*?

"I think I hurt my back," Rodney said.

Dolittle shook his head. "I'm dreaming," he said to himself. "I'm having a dream, a *very bad dream.*"

"Whoa, hold it, buddy," Rodney said. "You're talking and I'm hearing you. You're not dreaming."

"I can't be hearing you," Dolittle said to the guinea pig. "There must be—"

"All right, let's get a grip here," Rodney said.

"Right, a grip, right," Dolittle repeated. He stared

at the cage, then got out of the car. He hurried around to the passenger side and opened the door, grabbing the cage.

A woman who was walking along the road, carrying a basket, came over to him.

"Need any help?" she asked.

"Help?" Dolittle laughed. "No, no help. Thank you. I'm just . . . uh . . . we're just stretching our legs."

"Ask her if she has any lettuce in that basket," Rodney said.

"Shut up," Dolittle said to the cage. "Shut your furry little mouth." He looked at the woman and laughed. She stared at him as she heard him making rodent noises.

"You're sure you're okay?" she asked.

"Yeah, why?" Dolittle asked.

"Well," she said nervously, "you were . . . squeaking like a guinea pig."

"Is *that* what it sounded like?" he asked.

She clutched her basket and hurried across the road.

"So now what?" Rodney asked. Dolittle took a deep breath. He put the cage on the side of the road.

"Hey!" Rodney called. "What are you doing? It's hot out here! I'll roast! Don't leave me! I'm down on my little knees!"

Dolittle listened, turned, and jumped into the car.

He slammed the door, drove a short distance, then stopped, reversed, got out, and returned to the cage.

"Oh, man! You scared the heck out of me!" Rodney said.

Dolittle picked up the cage. "Shut up," he said. "If you say another word I'm leaving you in the road! I mean it!"

"Okay, okay," Rodney promised.

Dolittle looked around, trying to figure out what to do so that he wouldn't have to listen to Rodney for the whole drive. He walked to the back of the car, opened the rear door, and pulled out several bungee cords. "This ought to do it," he said. Moments later he was cruising on the highway, smiling and relaxed again, with the radio blasting. The cage was strapped to the roof rack and Rodney, his fur flattened by the wind, clung to the cage in terror.

everal hours later, Dolittle rounded a corner to the Big Bear Ranch. As he pulled up the long, winding driveway, Lisa and Dolittle's father, Archer Dolittle, were sitting at a picnic table, finishing lunch. Charisse lay in the sun near the water, her radio blaring. Maya had buried her head in a laptop computer.

Dolittle's car's radio outblasted his daughter's and startled the family. "I made it!" he called, hopping out of the car. Lisa, Archer, and Maya looked at him, shocked.

"Rodney!" Maya shrieked as she spotted the cage on the roof. Archer ran to help her get the cage down. "Daddy, how *could* you put Rodney up there?" she asked.

Dolittle shrugged. "Figured fresh air would do him good," he said. "Nice little rodent, huh?"

Lisa came over and hugged her husband. "I missed you," she said. "Tell me, how was your meeting?"

Dolittle shook his head. "Meeting? Oh, right, the meeting. Good. Good meeting."

Lisa stepped back and looked at him. "John, are you okay? You look a little frazzled."

"Frazzled? Me? No, no. Had a nice . . . quiet . . . drive up here," he said.

Maya passed with the guinea pig cage. "Lunatic!" Rodney shouted. Dolittle looked to see if anyone else had heard the pet talk to him. He breathed a huge sigh of relief when he realized they hadn't.

After dinner John and his father went outside to play horseshoes. Charisse sat nearby, talking on a cordless phone.

"That Calnet's a big outfit," Archer said to his son.

"Yeah. Huge." John Dolittle nodded.

"Seems if they're offering a good deal you might want to take it."

"Not just yet," Dolittle said. "We want to make sure it's the right company."

"You don't know how these big companies think," his father said. "They can get cold feet and leave you at the altar."

"They want us," Dolittle said.

"Hate to see you lose this one."

"I'm not going to lose it!" Dolittle replied testily. He pitched a horseshoe and went to retrieve it. As he picked it up, he noticed a rabbit staring at him. Dolittle tensed. The rabbit stared and hopped off. Dolittle returned to his father, who was watching Maya crawling on the ground.

"Maya, want to pitch a few?" her grandfather asked.

"No, thanks, I'm watching a praying mantis eat a ladybug," she said matter-of-factly.

"What for?" her grandfather asked.

"It's just a phase," Dolittle said, glancing at his father. "All kids go through it."

"You never did," Archer said as he looked at his son's horseshoe grip. "That's the wrong way to hold it, John."

"There is no wrong way!" Dolittle said. "There's just *ways—different* ways." Dolittle pitched his horseshoe. It fell nowhere near the post.

"Calnet made a big offer, huh?" his father said, getting back to the original subject.

"Yeah."

"Don't blow it, son." Archer threw a ringer, put his hands on his hips, and smiled. Maya came over to her father, holding up a bug.

"Daddy, what if I went *after* the chick is born?" she asked.

Dolittle looked at her. "Maya, you're going to camp *now*. I don't want to hear any more about it, okay?" he said sternly, and stormed off.

"What's eating him?" Maya asked her grandfather.

"Ignore him. It's just business stuff," Archer said.

Later that night, Lisa lay in bed reading. Dolittle came in and went into the bathroom, where he started brushing his teeth with a vengeance.

"I don't know why you let your father get to you like that, John," Lisa called.

Dolittle came out of the bathroom, his mouth full of toothpaste, and walked angrily across the bedroom, talking unintelligibly. He turned and went back to the bathroom, spit, rinsed his mouth, and returned to the bedroom.

"He does *not* get to me," he said calmly.

"Good," Lisa said. "Then c'mere and give me a hug. I've missed you!"

She hugged him and he kissed her. Then he sat up and said, "He was telling *me* how to pitch horseshoes!"

Lisa kissed him again, trying to take his mind off horseshoes.

"He had a leader, not a ringer!" he said angrily.

"I can see *you're* in a great mood," she sighed.

"I am. I am," he said, kissing her.

"Wait here," she said. "I'll be right back." She went to the bathroom.

Dolittle started to get into bed.

"Hello!" a voice called.

He froze.

"Over here!" the voice said, coming from the direction of the outside door. Slowly, nervously, Dolittle went to the door, opened it, and looked out. At first he saw nothing. Then the bright eyes of a huge owl in a tree stared him in the face. Dolittle gasped.

"Hello," the owl said again.

"Oh, God," Dolittle moaned.

"You're the one who can hear us, aren't you?"

"I don't hear anything," Dolittle protested.

"Listen," the owl said, "the whole woods are talkin' about you. Can you do me a favor? Can you just take this stick out of my wing? It's killing me!" He turned his head around 180 degrees. "Don't worry," the owl said. "I won't hurt you." Dolittle approached slowly and deftly removed the wood.

"Ahhhhhhhh, oh, much better. Oh . . . thank you!"

Dolittle went back inside and looked into the mirror next to the door. "What's happening to me?" he asked.

Lisa came back into the bedroom, smiling, and put her arms around John's neck. He jumped at her touch, staring at the owl, which was out of her view.

"Honey, I just want to spend some time with you," she said sweetly.

"I know," he said, grinning awkwardly and slamming the door shut. "I just need a glass of water. Be right back." He walked to the counter in the cabin's kitchen area. He reached for a glass, filled it with cold water from the water cooler, held it to his mouth, and then flung the water into his face.

"I gotta wake up from this nightmare," he said out loud. In the guinea pig cage on the floor, Rodney was running on his wheel, singing the words of a popular song.

Dolittle stood frozen, frightened because he could understand the guinea pig's squeaks. A raccoon that was sitting on the windowsill suddenly spoke up. "Can I make a request?" the raccoon asked, pointing to the boxes and cans of food in the cabin. "Can you get tuna in oil instead of water next time?"

Dolittle dropped the glass. It shattered on the floor and he ran out of the cabin into the yard.

"Breathe, breathe," he said to himself. Talking raccoons? Singing guinea pigs? What was going on?

"Hey, buddy," Dolittle heard someone call. He turned, looked in the direction of the voice, and spotted a possum.

"My old lady's on the warpath," the possum said in language clearly understandable to Dolittle. "If she asks you if you saw me, I was in that tree all night, get it?" He winked and scampered off.

Dolittle rubbed his face with both hands and staggered backward, tripping over something.

"Hey, that's my tail! You're on my tail!" a voice cried. Dolittle jumped back and stared into the face of a skunk. "Oh, it's you," the skunk said forgivingly. "I was ready to lock and load. It's a good thing I saw who did it." Dolittle felt himself begin to twitch nervously. He turned and faced the raccoon again. The raccoon was still on the subject of foodstuffs. "Or could you at least buy salmon?" the raccoon asked the near-hysterical Dolittle. "I'd *love* some salmon."

Suddenly Lisa called from the window. "John? Is that you outside?"

"Shut up!" Dolittle replied.

"What did you say to me?" she demanded, sticking her head out the window.

"I . . . I have to go back to the city," he stammered.

"When?

"Right now. *Immediately*," he said.

"*Now?* John, is something wrong?" she called.

"No, no, no! It's an emergency. I . . . dropped a glass in the kitchen. I'm coming in there to get dressed."

Back in the bedroom, Lisa followed him, looking at him fearfully.

"You dropped a glass so you need to go back to the city?" she asked incredulously.

"Yeah," he said, pulling his jeans over his pajamas

and a sweatshirt over his head. "I'm gonna go get the good broom from home."

"John," Lisa said, looking worried, "are you sure you're all right? Did something happen that you want to talk about? The contract? Maya's camp? Anything?"

Dolittle gathered clothes haphazardly in his arms. "No, see, um, it's an emergency. I have to see a doctor—I mean, I *am* a doctor. I got beeped. It's an emergency," he rattled on. He walked outside, carrying his clothes. Lisa followed.

"But I thought you had this weekend off and some other doctor was covering your patients for you," she said. "You were on last weekend, remember?"

"Um, yeah, um . . . That's who's sick—the other doctor—so I gotta go."

"John, this is crazy," Lisa said, starting to to get angry. "Don't you dare go driving out of here in the middle of the night!"

Dolittle looked away from her. "You're right, it's nuts. But, honey, you've been a doctor's wife long enough to know how crazy the schedules can be. I'll be back. Gotta go!" He kissed her, jumped into the car, and drove off, right over a pile of horseshoes.

He raced down the windy road at breakneck speed, talking to himself. "Gotta see somebody about all these talking animals. Gotta get over this!" He drove back to San Francisco, made a call on his car phone to his friend Dr. Scott Sherman, then raced across the Golden Gate Bridge and drove straight to his office building. He pulled up in front of the locked building and skidded to a stop in the dark parking lot.

Dolittle jumped out of the car and raced up and down the street, looking for his friend. As he approached an alley down the street from the building, he heard voices coming from a large Dumpster.

"This is bull!" one voice said.

"What's your problem?" a second voice replied.

"Your face, man! There's nothing in here but paper. I came here to *eat*, not *read*, stupid."

Slowly Dolittle peeked around the corner and spotted two rats in the garbage.

"Oh, no!" Dolittle groaned.

The rats' conversation continued, and Dolittle listened.

"Don't start with me. I'll hit you so hard you'll see ten more of me," the first one said.

"Yeah? Come on with it," his buddy answered.

"Oh, man, you are tempting fate now," the first rat said; then he looked up and spotted Dolittle. "Hey— what are *you* looking at, buster?"

"Me? Uh . . ." Dolittle couldn't speak.

"*Uh . . . ,*" the rat said, making fun of him. "Can't you talk?"

"I'm looking at two greasy-looking rats fighting over some garbage," Dolittle said, shaking his head.

"Come in *here* and say that," one rat challenged. "We'll gnaw your bottom for a week."

Dolittle leaned over the Dumpster. "Yeah? Well, you better pray *I* don't come in there, Mighty Mouse, or I'll turn you *both* into slippers."

The rat jumped. "Oh? And how about I take this lightbulb, stick it in your mouth, and turn *you* into a lamp?"

Dolittle started really getting into the fight. "How about I take *your* tail, jam it up your nose, pull it out your mouth, and poke your eyes out with it?" He laughed.

Suddenly the shadow of another man was visible at the end of the alley. "John?" Dr. Scott Sherman called. "Is that you?"

Dolittle turned. As he recognized his friend, Dolittle looked embarrassed. "Oh! Scott! *Hi* . . . thanks for coming."

"Who were you talking to?" Sherman asked curiously.

"Um . . . just a couple of rats," Dolittle said. "Actually, that's why I wanted to see you, Scott," he added. The doctor unlocked the medical building and led Dolittle to the radiology office on the first floor.

Dr. Sherman shook his head but remained silent as they entered the office.

"Now, let's take those X rays and see what's going on," Sherman said.

A short time later, Dolittle and Sherman stood next to the lighted screen displaying X rays of Dolittle's brain.

"No shadows, nothing unusual showing up," Sherman said.

"What is wrong with me, then?" Dolittle asked. "Look, Scott, I don't want to become one of those guys you see on the street talking to themselves."

"Have you been under any unusual stress lately?" Sherman asked.

"No. Well . . ." Dolittle hesitated, then said in a rush, "Actually, yes. You see there's the *Calnet* sale and— Oh! And I'm forcing my daughter to go to camp, and even though I'm sure I'm right about it, I'm feeling some guilt about it and, um, I hit a dog with my car."

"You *hit* a dog?" Sherman said.

"Scott, don't make me feel worse than I already do, for God's sake," Dolittle said.

"Sorry. But a dog . . . ?"

"I didn't kill him. He ran off," Dolittle added.

"Injured?"

"He was well enough to call me bonehead, if you can believe that," Dolittle explained.

"John, the dog couldn't have said anything," Sherman said. He stood back and stared hard at Dolittle.

"He called me bonehead! I heard it," Dolittle said.

"John, believe me, the dog did *not* talk to you," Sherman said slowly and deliberately.

Dolittle shook his head. "You're right, you're right. Probably just stress, right?"

"Right," Sherman assured him. "You'll be fine. Just take it easy for a couple of days."

"Thanks, Scott," Dolittle said. "By the way, if you didn't know me and I just came in off the street, what would your diagnosis be?"

Sherman looked him straight in the eye. "I'd think you were going a bit crazy," he said without hesitation.

olittle decided to head back to the Big Bear Ranch and drove along the dark, empty streets. He dialed Lisa.

"Hello?" Lisa answered, sounding groggy.

"Hey, sweetie," Dolittle said brightly. "Did I wake you?"

"Of course you woke me," she grumbled. "Do you know what time it is? John, where *are* you? Are you okay?"

"I'm fine. Honey, I am *so* sorry," he said. "I just kinda lost my head there a little bit. I'm really okay. I'm on my way now. Be there soon. Love you."

He hung up the phone and stopped at a traffic light behind a dogcatcher's truck. John looked in the back and saw a vaguely familiar mixed-breed dog staring at him.

"Bonehead!" the mutt yelled. The light turned green and the truck pulled away.

Dolittle sat frozen as he watched the truck disappear into the dark.

"I didn't see a dog and I didn't hear a dog call to me," he said. "I'm just tired. This is a bad dream." There were no cars behind him, and he saw that the light had turned red again.

The sun rose in the sky. Dolittle spotted a sign with an arrow that read ANIMAL SHELTER and followed it without thinking. He parked the car and got out, hearing the barking of dogs and the yelping of other animals. He tried not to pay attention to what they were saying.

He walked up the steps to the shelter, opened the screen door, and walked in.

"I'm here to look for a dog that just came in," he said to a woman sitting behind a desk.

"Through those doors," she said, pointing to the right. Dolittle stood frozen, unable to follow her directions. "Can I show you the way?" the woman asked, looking at him strangely. When he didn't answer, she rose and walked toward the door. Dolittle followed without saying a word. As he passed into the kennels he was overcome with panic. Hundreds of dogs were barking and yapping. Dolittle understood everything they said! The dogs were speaking to him!

39

"Take me! I do tricks! Look at this," a black husky called. "I'm housebroken! I don't shed, I don't shed!"

Dolittle walked by a cage inside which a small, tough-looking bulldog stood looking at him.

"You want anyone killed? Say the word and their guts are in your driveway," the dog said. Just then Dolittle spotted another woman leading away the mutt who had called him bonehead.

"Dead dog walkin'," a rottweiler called out.

"He's a goner," added the bulldog.

The rottweiler shook his head. "It's Gas City for that one."

Dolittle hurried after the woman. The mutt pleaded, "Wait, wait, I have owners. They've just been out of town for a few years."

As they passed an office, a phone rang and the woman pulled the dog inside to answer it.

"That might be the warden!" the mutt cried. "Maybe I'm saved by the bell."

The woman hung up and walked the dog over to Dolittle. "I've been informed you want this guy." she said matter-of-factly. "You sure? He's a temperamental old thing."

"Yeah, yeah," Dolittle said, smiling sheepishly. "I've got a soft spot for old dogs. He's just what my daughter's been asking for. She'll shape him up."

"It's your choice," she said, handing the leash over

to Dolittle. The dog leaped up and licked his face, his tail wagging furiously.

"That's the happiest I've ever seen this mutt." The woman laughed. "Maybe you're a good match." She smiled and turned away. "Good luck!"

Dolittle walked out of the shelter.

The dog barked at his new friend. "Hey, hey! Thanks a lot," he said. "Whoa, that was close! About as close as I ever got to the Big Room. Whew! Hope you've really got kids. I love kids! Kids are the greatest!"

"Yeah, yeah, kids are good," Dolittle said. "What's going on?"

"You understood me? Weird! Most people can't," the dog said.

"No kidding," Dolittle replied. "I must be going nuts. Why can I hear animals talking?"

The dog looked at Dolittle closely. "Because you care," the dog said softly.

"What!" Dolittle exclaimed, staring at the animal. "I don't care. I just want to stop hearing voices. I want to get on with my life! I think I'm cracking up!"

The dog sat down on the pavement, forcing Dolittle to stop. "I've heard of this happening before," he explained. "It's like you tapped into our frequency or something."

Dolittle sighed and shook his head. "No way!

You're not a radio, you're a mammal. And mammals don't talk!"

"*Nooooo,* right!" the dog said sarcastically. "I forgot. Only you *humans* speak. Only the upright have the precious *gift* of communication. What the heck do you think barking is? An involuntary spasm? Animals *do* talk. It's nothing new or revolutionary. You just haven't been listening . . . until now."

Dolittle tugged at the dog's leash, heading toward the car. "I must be having some sort of extended dream or breakdown," he said, wiping the sweat from his forehead. He reached down and released the leash from the collar. "So long," he said to the dog. "Good luck." He started to get into the car.

The dog jumped up on him. "*Good luck?* That's it? You're just gonna walk? You almost killed me with that car. Hit and run, man."

Dolittle pushed him gently down and away from the car. "And now I saved you," he said. "We're even."

The dog started sneezing, weaving around as if he was sick and dizzy. Dolittle got into the car, trying to ignore him, but the dog gave the show of his life. He spun around, coughing and sneezing, and fell to the ground. "Oh, oh, maybe it's that truck exhaust," the dog moaned. "Oh my God. Everything's going black. But don't worry, I'm fine, really. Must be my allergies. Oh, no! My head! The pain!" He collapsed on his back, legs in the air.

"Oh my God," Dolittle cried. He jumped from the car and lifted the dog, putting him in the backseat. He put his ear to the dog's side, listening for a pulse. "He's still alive. I have to find a vet."

Dolittle jumped into the car. The dog rolled over and made himself comfortable in the backseat. The good old fake-sick routine. He winked as Dolittle sped off from the shelter.

Dolittle called Information from his car phone and got the name and address of a veterinary clinic.

"Hey, how you doing back there?" Dolittle called.

"Better, thanks," the dog said. "Just having a little trouble breathing. Could you open the window or turn up the air?"

Dolittle turned up the air-conditioning. At a fork in the road he followed the arrow to the vet's and pulled up in front of a huge building.

"Let's go," he called. The dog was now sitting up in the backseat, enjoying the cool air, feeling perfectly fine.

They walked into the clinic, which was filled with animals and their owners. People sat with dogs on leashes, cats in boxes, birds in cages. One parrot stood sluggishly on his owner's shoulder. Dolittle went to the receptionist at the desk.

"May I help you?" she asked.

"Dolittle. I called a few minutes ago from my car phone. It's an emergency."

"Everyone has an emergency." She smiled. "Please have a seat."

Dolittle sat down on one of the few empty chairs. The mutt sat happily on the floor in front of him, eyeing a cute little poodle on the other side of the room.

A heavy set woman waddled to the door with a dog on a leash. "Is that the biggest bottom you've ever seen?" the dog asked Dolittle, nodding at the woman as she jerked his leash and pulled him out the door.

Dolittle turned to the old woman sitting next to him. She was yelling at her old beagle. "Chauncy, sit! Chauncy!" she hollered. "He's deaf," she explained to Dolittle.

"Deaf? I'm not deaf," the beagle told Dolittle. "I just can't stand listening to that voice!"

The mutt looked up at Dolittle. "Poor sucker," he said. Dolittle grinned.

"Dolittle," the nurse called. The doctor grabbed the mutt's leash and led him into the exam room.

The vet, Dr. Fish, was a short, stout balding man. He patted the examination table and the dog jumped up.

"So, what seems to be the problem?" he asked.

"I suspect pulmonary distress. Maybe fluid on the lungs," Dolittle said in a professional manner.

"Oh," Dr. Fish said, laughing sarcastically. "You must be a doctor for *people.*"

"Yes, I am," Dolittle said.

Fish smirked. "I can always tell when a *real* doctor brings in an animal," he said not attempting to hide his contempt. "They always like to do a little amateur diagnosing." He lifted one of the dog's rear legs.

The mutt barked. "Could you tell him to get away from my bottom?" he said to Dolittle. "I know *one* thing. I have *no* fluid in my butt."

About an hour later Dolittle and the mutt walked into the waiting room. The dog moaned dramatically, "Ohhh. Ohhh. *Oh* . . . Ohhh."

Dolittle paid the receptionist.

Fish came into the waiting room and started talking to Dolittle. While listening to him, Dolittle heard the talking of the animals still waiting to be treated.

Dolittle put his arm around the vet and pointed at the animals in the waiting room. "Let me save you some time here, Doc," he said. "That dog has nothing wrong with his stomach; he just hates his owner's cooking. That puppy has an ear infection. And all that's wrong with that poodle is that the groomer put her collar on too tight." Dolittle smiled. Fish stood with his mouth hanging open.

Dolittle led the mutt out the door and back to the car. He drove along the country roads, taking deep breaths, trying to clear his head and figure out what to do.

The mutt moaned.

"What's wrong?" Dolittle asked.

"Everything's going by so fast. I'm gettin' dizzy . . ."

"Don't you dare throw up in this car," Dolittle ordered. "What are you looking at?"

"The lines on the road, mostly," the mutt said, "they're just whipping by. Line, line, line, line—they're making me sick."

"Don't focus on them," Dolittle ordered. "Look at the buildings. And *don't* get sick!"

"Okay, okay," the dog groaned. He leaned his head out the open window. "Building, building, building, building—this is worse than the lines," he said. "It's not working. Building, building, building. This is making me crazy!"

He lifted his paw and accidentally dropped it down on the automatic window button. The window rose, trapping the dog's head. He gagged and sputtered, unable to speak. When Dolittle saw him in the rearview mirror, he quickly opened the window with the front control. The dog coughed. Dolittle screeched the car to a halt on the side of the road.

"All right! That's it!" Dolittle ordered. "Out. Hit the road."

"What? I thought I was your pet."

Dolittle waved his hands. "No, thank you. I don't want a pet. I already have a large egg and a guinea pig to worry about. And if I did want a pet, I wouldn't want one as annoying as you." He stood by the car and opened the door. The dog jumped out and walked sadly up the road. "Nice guy, very kind," the mutt muttered as he shuffled slowly along. "Hey, don't worry about me. I'll just be going down the road, disappearing without a trace."

Suddenly Dolittle's car phone rang. He climbed into the car, leaving the back door open.

"Hello?"

"John? You called in the middle of the night and said you were coming right home!" Lisa shouted. "We're about to take Maya to camp."

"I'll meet you there. Something else came up," Dolittle said, his voice exhausted.

"Hold on, Maya wants to talk to you," Lisa said, handing the phone to Maya.

"Hi, Daddy," Maya said, sounding sad.

"Hi, honey, how are you?"

"I'm fine, I guess," she said, sniffling dramatically. "Am I going to see you before I go to camp?"

The mutt walked back toward the car as Dolittle talked on the phone.

"I'll meet you there," Dolittle said. The mutt started barking loudly.

Dolittle covered the phone. "Would you stop that?" he whispered at the dog.

"Daddy, is that a dog?" Maya asked excitedly.

"Yes, honey, but it's—"

The mutt barked and barked.

Dolittle covered the mouthpiece of the phone. "Shut up!" he shouted at the dog.

"Daddy?" Maya asked excitedly. "Did you get me a dog? Oh, I love you! Mommy, guess what! Daddy got me a dog!"

"No, Maya, I—" Dolittle began.

"Honey?" Lisa was back on the phone. "Is that what you've been doing? How wonderful! You little sneak!" She laughed.

"Grandpa!" Dolittle heard Maya calling in the background. "Daddy got me a dog! Isn't that fabulous?"

Dolittle shot a mean look at the mutt, who suddenly was walking happily up and down the road. The dog hopped into the backseat. "What? What?" The mutt said innocently. "I'm a dog. I'm supposed to bark!"

Dolittle hung up the phone and slammed the rear door shut. He got back behind the wheel. "I guess now I have to keep you," he mumbled, noticing the dog's remarkable recovery.

6

Dolittle raced along, heading toward Camp Hawkeye, where Maya was to spend four weeks. The dog chatted happily in the backseat, asking Dolittle about the family, how old his daughters were, and what his house was like.

"This is really exciting, Doc," the mutt said. "First I get saved from the death chamber, then I find out you can understand animal talk, and now I learn you're a doctor with kids! I can't wait to meet everybody. What a great day!"

"We're almost there," Dolittle said. "Two more miles. Your new family's going to want to know your name." He shook his head in disbelief at the whole conversation.

"I don't have one," the mutt said.

"Well, think of one. What would you like to be called?"

"A little girl called me, Please, Mommy, Not Him. How about that?"

"How about Lucy?" Dolittle suggested.

"Lucy, yes. I like that. *Lucy,* that's a good, solid name. There's just one problem," the dog said. *"I'm a guy!"*

"Oh, right," Dolittle said. "Hmmm . . . "How about—Lucky?"

"Perfect!" the dog yelped. "*Lucky.* Yes. I like it. 'Hi, I'm Lucky! How're you?' It works on *two* levels, Doc! I love it!"

Dolittle reached the camp and pulled his car next to Lisa's van. He got out with Lucky, spotted the family, and waved. Maya waved back and raced over to greet them.

"Hi, doggie!" she said, hugging Lucky as he wagged his tail happily.

"His name's Lucky," her father said.

"Lucky! How great!" She hugged him again. "Oh, Daddy, he's perfect. I love him!"

"Right back at you, honey," Lucky said, barking happily. "I could learn to like this family stuff."

"So, let's go see your bunk, Maya," Dolittle said as he walked toward the cabins.

"I *really* don't know if I want to stay, Daddy," Maya said, hesitating.

"Okay," her father said. "Here's the deal. You stay here at camp, you have a really great time, and then Lucky's all yours!"

Lisa came out of Maya's cabin. "I think you're all set, honey," she said. "Charisse did a really great job with your cubbies."

"Four weeks is a long time," Maya said, her bottom lip quivering.

Her father lifted her into the air and spun her around, forcing her to laugh. "Hey, kiddo, it'll go by before you know it. You'll see. You'll thank me when you're older and have tons of friends."

Lisa and Dolittle hugged Maya, trying to give her confidence. Two older girls walked by, stared at Maya's shoes, and laughed. A small tear trickled down Maya's face. Her parents didn't notice. Maya hugged them hard, wishing she could leave.

The bell rang to signal that all family members had to say goodbye. Maya stood at the parking lot gate waving until the counselors herded the girls into the social hall. Lisa and Charisse drove off in the van to the city.

Dolittle looked down at Lucky and opened the back door of his car. "Okay, boy, in you go."

Lucky hopped into the backseat, stretched out, and was soon fast asleep.

Dolittle looked at him and couldn't help smiling. "Well, at least I won't be talking to an animal for a while," he said. He followed the country roads that led to the highway and back to San Francisco. The sun was setting as he crossed the Golden Gate Bridge. He sped across the bridge and over the hilly streets of the city to his apartment building.

He pulled the car into the spot next to Lisa's. She and Charisse were already home. When the car stopped, Lucky jumped up and started barking.

"Okay, we're home," Dolittle said.

After dinner, Paprika—as she reminded her father she was to be called—took Lucky into her room, where she said he could sleep until he found the right spot for himself.

"I'm wiped!" Dolittle said as he finished drying the last pot and headed into the bedroom. He plopped on the bed without even taking off the spread. Lisa came in and snuggled beside him.

"Crazy day," he said, holding her, "just a crazy day."

The doorbell rang and Lucky started barking. "Be right back," Dolittle said as he got up and went to the door. "Don't go away."

The bell rang again.

"Hold your horses," he said. He opened the door and his mouth dropped open. Three sheep stood outside the door looking up at him. He closed the door, hoping he had seen a mirage. Then he heard strange sounds coming from the kitchen.

There he found a group of large ducks, who had come in through the terrace door. They were making themselves at home on the counter. He shooed them back out just as the doorbell rang again.

As he walked to the door, he grabbed a long umbrella from the umbrella stand.

"Get out . . . ," he started to say, expecting to see the sheep.

His partner Mark Weller entered. Dolittle peeked down the building hallway and spotted the sheep hiding in the corner. He closed the door and went inside.

"I got him. You owe me, buddy," Weller said to Dolittle. "I just came back from drinks with Gene. Many drinks, actually, and the good news is he's in."

"Okay. Well, that's good, great! Very, very good, Mark. Now good-night," Dolittle said, trying to get Weller to the door.

"Now I've just got to know if we've got *you*," Weller said. "You were downright screwy at the meeting. I covered for you, of course, but . . ."

Dolittle looked behind Weller and saw a goat cross the living room. He blinked. "A goat," he said, shaking his head.

"A *goat*?" Weller repeated.

"Don't make *me* the goat, Mark," Dolittle said. "I'm in, man. You know I'm in." He tried to ignore the strange sounds coming from the other room.

"There's something strange in your kitchen," Weller said. "Did you leave the terrace door open?"

"A dog," Dolittle said, stopping Weller before he could go into the room. "We got a new dog. For Maya. A going-away present so she'd go to camp."

"That doesn't sound like a dog," Weller said, trying to get around Dolittle.

"A *pound* dog, very neurotic, makes weird noises," Dolittle explained. "Thanks for dropping by. You really have to get going." He led Weller to the apartment door. The doorbell rang.

Dolittle blocked Weller. "Wait," Dolittle said. "Don't go."

"Are you expecting someone?" Weller asked.

"My umbrella," Dolittle said. "My neighbor wanted to borrow an umbrella. Wait here, and *don't move!*"

Dolittle slipped out the apartment door with the umbrella and closed it behind himself. Weller stood alone inside the apartment, frozen in place, until he heard something strange from the kitchen. He was inching toward the kitchen door when suddenly Lucky sprang down the hall and leaped up on him, pushing him away from the kitchen door.

Dolittle reentered through the front door after herding the sheep back to the corner of the hallway and tossing the umbrella down the hall's mail chute. He went to his dog. "Down, boy. Good boy. Good boy! Coast is clear. Okay, so, good-night, Mark. And thanks for coming by. You can count on me. I'm as solid as a rock," Dolittle told his fellow doctor.

"Great," Weller said, patting Lucky's head. "Nice doggie. I'll call Calloway first thing tomorrow. We're gonna be rich. Rich. *Rich!*"

Dolittle smiled and pushed Weller into the hall.

"Rich, yes. Good-night, Mark." Dolittle shut the door. When he turned, he saw the ducks waddling from the kitchen toward the bathroom and the goat heading for his bedroom.

"Stop the ducks!" he whispered to Lucky. "I'll get the goat."

He chased the goat around the corner, pushed it behind him, and leaned in the bedroom doorway.

"What's going on out there?" Lisa asked from the bedroom.

"That was Mark—*owww!*" John said as the goat nibbled on his socks. "I'm gonna have to work on the deal. I'm gonna be up late—*hey!*"

Lisa stared at him. "John Dolittle, I don't know what has gotten into you!" She scowled. "I'll see you in the morning. I'll be the one cooking breakfast." She turned off her lamp and pulled up the covers.

Dolittle frowned. "Oh, honey, don't be like that— down, Lucky! Dog's biting me. I gotta walk him. Hey—" He withdrew back into the hallway and shut the door. He walked the goat down the hall.

"What next?" he whispered. He spotted Charisse coming down the hall toward the bathroom.

"Freeze!" he said. "What are you doing up?"

She stopped. "Have to go to the bathroom. What're you doing?"

"Nothing," he said nonchalantly. "Hold on," he added as he quickly tied the goat to the leg of a table in the hall. The goat secured, he moved toward his daughter.

"Go back to bed. You're old enough to hold it in," he said.

He opened the bathroom door and peeked in. Lucky had the ducks in the bathtub and was drawing the shower curtain closed.

Charisse rolled her eyes. "Dad, are you nuts or something? I have to go!"

"Lucky's using it," Dolittle said.

"A dog is using the bathroom?" She looked at him strangely. "What kind of dog is this?"

"A smart dog," Dolittle answered. "A very, very smart and clean dog."

Just then they both heard the toilet flushing, and Lucky came out of the bathroom with a piece of toilet paper stuck to his paw.

Charisse stared in amazement. Dolittle and Lucky exchanged glances of relief.

"Okay," Dolittle said. "Your turn. Just let me make sure he left the seat down."

He went into the bathroom and glared at the ducks in the bathtub. "Not one quack," he said to them. "Got it?" The ducks nodded. He drew the shower curtain tighter around the tub as Charisse entered.

Dolittle stood in front of the shower curtain. "I don't need adult supervision, Dad," she said.

Dolittle reluctantly left the bathroom, and Charisse closed the door.

Down the hallway, the goat was dragging the table behind it. "Get out of my house!" Dolittle whispered at the goat. Lucky helped him untie the animal, and they slowly pushed it toward the front door.

As Charisse came out of the bathroom, she walked down the hall to her room. "Good night, Dad," she called, unable to see the goat. Her father smiled as if nothing was happening.

"Oh, good night, honey. Sweet dreams!" he said.

Charisse went into her room and closed the door. Just as Dolittle opened the front door to push out the goat, the sheep marched in, heading for the kitchen. They were followed by more animals, who walked through the front door, filed right past a terror-stricken Dolittle, and proceeded into the kitchen.

Dolittle waved his arms. "Hey, *sure,* come on in," he said sarcastically. "Make yourself at home. There's chips and dips, fresh vegetables, barbecued chicken. You name it!"

When the last animal was in, Dolittle closed the door and leaned against it, his head in his hands.

The beautiful modern kitchen looked like a barnyard.

"What is this?" Dolittle said as he looked around what had become an animal waiting room. "What's going on?"

"Referrals," the owl said, explaining that the animals had come to be treated by the famous Dolittle, who could understand and speak to them all. "Word is you're a doctor who cares," the owl explained.

Lucky wagged his tail in agreement. "They need you, Doc."

Dolittle looked around the room again, then rolled up his sleeves. "I can't believe I'm doing his," he said. "All right. Who's first?"

Several hours later he was still treating the animals. He examined a goat's udder. Next to him was his

Doctor Dolittle (Eddie Murphy).

Maya (Kyla Pratt) comforts Rodney (voice of Chris Rock).

Dolittle has a discussion with Lucky (voice of Norm MacDonald).

Lisa (Corrine Boucher) and Maya Dolittle with Lucky.

Something grabs Lucky's attention.

The invasion of the animals! The kitchen looks like a barnyard when the animals come to Dolittle for medical advice.

Dolittle counsels two troubled pigeons (voices of Julie Kavner and Gary Shandling).

"Let's try this," Dolittle says as he slips the makeshift glasses onto the face of the horse (voice of Dennis Franz).

Inside the examination room, Dolittle evaluates the sick rat lying on the table.

A rat (voice of John Leguizamo) argues with Dolittle about his sick friend (voice of Reni Santoni).

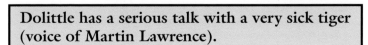

Dolittle has a serious talk with a very sick tiger (voice of Martin Lawrence).

The egg hatches and Rodney investi- gates. "Mama," the baby alligator calls the guinea pig.

Maya, Rodney, and Lucky inspect the broken shell.

medical bag and a box filled with samples of medicine that he kept at home.

"Okay," he said to the goat. "This should take care of that irritation. I'll put some on now, but the problem is who's gonna do it for you three times a day?"

"Excuse me," a voice called. "Is this where the doctor is?"

Dolittle went to the window. Down below, a police horse craned his neck toward the terrace.

"Yeah," Dolittle sighed. "That's me."

"What's your location, there, Doc?" the horse called loudly.

"I'm up here," Dolittle called. "Right above you."

"Ah, jeez, sorry," the horse yelled. "I don't see too good."

"No problem," Dolittle said. "But could you keep your voice down just a little?"

"Oh, yeah, sure, Doc," the horse said, speaking just as loudly as before. "I'm with the San Francisco P.D. equine unit. Got ten years in, but now they're talking about putting me out to pasture. I need your help."

Later that night, Dolittle sat at the kitchen counter with his toolbox, fastening together two magnifying glasses and some wire, fashioning a strange-looking pair of eyeglasses. He picked up the glasses and his doctor's bag, took the elevator down to the lobby, and went outside, where the horse stood waiting patiently.

"Let's try this," Dolittle said as he slipped the makeshift glasses onto the horse's face. "There. How's that?"

"Holy smokes!" the horse shouted. "I can see again. I can really see! Thanks a million, Doc."

"You're welcome," Dolittle said, smiling. He waved as the horse galloped down the street, looking all around. "My God," the horse said. "This is a beautiful city!"

On his way back inside, Dolittle saw a cat with a torn paw. He immediately began stitching the paw with a needle and surgical thread from his bag.

"How'd you do this?" Dolittle asked.

"Alley cat jumped me," the cat replied.

"Why?"

The cat shrugged. "I've been seeing his sister and she's a calico and I'm a tabby," he said.

"So?" Dolittle asked.

"So he doesn't think I'm good enough for his sister," the cat answered.

"Okay," the doctor said, shaking his head. "You're done. Be careful out there."

"Thanks, man," the cat said. "Say, if you really want to help somebody, you should go check out the biggest cat of them all. Word is he's in a real bad way."

"Where is he?" Dolittle asked.

The cat raised a paw, pointing to a circus poster hung on a lamppost.

Dolittle got Lucky, then drove across town to a large open field covered with huge tents. Colorful flags flew all around, and big posters featuring the special events were hung on every tree. Behind the tents were rows of animal cages.

Dolittle parked the car, and he and Lucky walked toward the tiger cages.

Lucky spoke up. "I think you should know, I'm not real good with big cats. They kind of freak me out."

"Just heel. Stay close and you'll be fine," the doctor said as he looked around, trying to find the cat section among the cages. They passed a baby tiger.

"Oh, he's not so big," Lucky said, sounding relieved.

Dolittle smiled. "That's not him, pal. That's the baby tiger." They kept walking until they found the cage of the adult tiger. Lucky backed up, but Dolittle walked forward.

The tiger was talking, practicing a routine. "Step, turn, growl, hiss, soft and sexy—then stop—" He spotted Dolittle and Lucky.

"Excu—" Dolittle started to say, when the huge tiger suddenly jumped back with a roar.

"*Jeez!*" the tiger growled. "Don't sneak up on me like that!"

"Sorry," Dolittle said.

"You understood me?" the tiger said in astonishment.

"Yes. I can talk to animals," Dolittle replied. "It's an honor to meet you. You've got a lot of fans. I've heard great things about you."

"You should have seen me in the old days," the tiger said sadly. "I was the first to jump through a flaming hoop, you know."

"Hey," Dolittle said, recalling a visit to the circus. "I think I did see you. When I was a kid. Did you ever play the Oakland Coliseum?"

"I played 'em all," the tiger said proudly. "I was the main cat until they started using those tacky Siberians. All white, blue eyes. What's with that? Are those even tigers?"

"Sounds like house cats," Dolittle said.

"House cats, exactly!" the tiger agreed.

"Kittens!" Dolittle laughed.

"Pussycats!" the tiger laughed along with him. His laugh turned into a deep cough, and he sat down, suddenly feeling weak.

Dolittle sat on a stepstool next to him. "Word on the street is you aren't feeling that well."

The tiger shook his head. "No, no, I'm fine. Tonight was just one of those things."

"What happened tonight?" Dolittle asked.

"Well, I got dizzy," the tiger said, looking at Dolittle. "It was the grand finale, where I jump onto the giant disco ball. You know, the one with all those tiny mirrors on it. Well, I was center stage, the spotlight was on, and I was alive! What a feeling! So I take my leap . . . and next thing I know I'm on my butt and the horses are laughing at me." He paused and lowered his head. "It was humiliating."

Dolittle shook his head. "Hey, those horses were just jealous of you. You're the headliner, they're the chorus line."

"You're a wise man," the tiger said. "Are you in show business?"

"Actually," Dolittle said slowly, "I'm a doctor!"

"Doctor?" the tiger said anxiously, jumping to his feet. "What is this? I'm fine. I don't need a doctor. It was nothing."

"Easy, easy, don't get upset," Dolittle said, trying to calm him. "I'm here as a friend. I want to help."

"Look, the best help you can give me is to get lost," the tiger said. "I appreciate your concern. But if they find out I'm sick, it's over. No more spotlight, no more center stage, and that's where I belong. That's where I *live*. And without it, I'll die."

"I know," Dolittle said. "I've seen you perform. I just want you to feel better. Maybe I can help."

"You're a dear, sweet man," the tiger said. "But

please, please, stay out of my way or I'll have to tear you apart and eat you!"

Dolittle patted his back. "Okay, pal," he said. "But if you change your mind, just let me know." Dolittle turned and walked away, and Lucky followed. The tiger went back to his rehearsing. Dolittle and Lucky passed the elephant cage.

The elephant called to Dolittle, "Hey, Doc. I've heard him mumbling about losing feeling on his right side. And sometimes he can't even pick up his head. I'm worried about him."

"Thanks for that information," Dolittle said to the elephant.

Dolittle led Lucky to the trainer's trailer and knocked on a door. After a moment the door opened and a tall, surly, barrel-chested man stood before them.

"Hi," Dolittle said. "I don't mean to bother you—"

"What do you want?" the animal trainer demanded.

"Do you take care of the tiger?"

"Yes! I am Oskar, the trainer!"

"Well, he's sick," Dolittle said.

Oskar started to close the trailer door. "The tiger is not sick, he is just old. As soon as I find a replacement I will put him down."

Dolittle put his foot in the door to keep it open.

"Put him down?" he asked. "Why? What if his illness is treatable?"

"He has been seen by a vet," Oskar said.

"But he didn't tell the vet his symptoms," Dolittle said.

Oskar laughed in Dolittle's face. "Who sent you? The clowns? Please, no jokes. Go! I must rest." He slammed the door in Dolittle's face.

Lucky growled. "Showpeople!"

The next day Dolittle went to work and began researching tigers. He sat at his office desk, looking through several thick textbooks that lay open in front of him. On a notepad he jotted down facts, going back and forth from book to book, checking and rechecking information.

He heard a knock at the door. "Come in," he called.

Mark Weller walked in. "I came to tell you that Jeremy Carson from Calnet called," he said jubilantly. "They upped the offer—more money!"

"Great," Dolittle said, only half listening. He continued to read his books.

"Don't forget," Weller said. "We're due over there, and Calloway wants to show us off tomorrow at some investor-shareholder thing."

"Fine," Dolittle said without looking up.

Weller looked at the book titles. "*Treating Big Cats?*" he asked.

"Maya's got a little kitten," Dolittle explained.

"Huh?" Weller said, looking confused.

Dolittle put down his notebook and pad and leaned back in his chair. He took a deep breath and looked at Weller. "Remember when we started out in that crummy little office in that miserable neighborhood? Making almost no money?" he asked seriously.

Weller shook his head. "I've blocked it out. What a nightmare."

"No," Dolittle said. "There was something about that time and place . . . an excitement. I couldn't wait to get to work. I'd wake up and think, 'Who am I gonna help today?' "

Dolittle looked at Weller, who didn't understand him at all. "Back then I know we made a difference," Dolittle said. "Last night I had to treat . . . some emergencies. And it was difficult. I was challenged. And it made me realize that I haven't been paying enough attention to my patients." He paused and looked at a framed photo of his family on the desk. "And maybe I haven't been paying attention at home either," he added.

Weller sighed and picked up a book from Dolittle's desk titled *Surgical Procedures for Tigers*.

"Got her a little Siamese." Dolittle flashed a big smile. "Named her Pookie."

Weller put the book down and frowned. "Hmmm . . . really . . . Well, anyway, the meeting's at three o'clock, John." He went out the door.

Dolittle buzzed for the secretary, who came right in. "Yes, Doctor?" she said.

"Diane, I need you to do me a favor. Locate a Dr. Louis Fish. He's a vet."

"I'm sure there must be a directory," Diane suggested. "Does it say where he's located?"

Dolittle picked up one of the books and opened the cover. "Let's see if it's in front here," he said as he flipped through a couple of pages. He stopped when he spotted something.

"Never mind, thanks, Diane. I think I've got it," he said, looking at a photograph of the smiling Dr. Fish.

He picked up the phone, asked Information for the number, and dialed. The nurse put him through to Fish.

"Is this Dr. Louis Fish, author of *Cat Illnesses and Diseases*?" Dolittle asked.

"Yes, it is," Fish said. "You've read my book?"

"But of course!" Dolittle said. "We keep it next to the bed. It's our Bible!"

"Well, some people do call it the definitive work on cats, but Bible?" Fish said slowly. "Well, actually I *could* see that. What can I do for you?"

Dolittle explained that a tiger at the circus was ill and asked if he could consult with Fish as he examined the animal.

"Well, of course, I'd be happy to help with a circus animal," Fish said, thinking he was talking to the tiger's vet.

"Great," Dolittle said. "I'm on my way there now. I'll call you back in about an hour."

Dolittle hung up, grabbed his notepad and a book, and raced out the door.

He arrived at the circus and immediately went to the big tiger's cage.

"Hey, how you doing?" Dolittle said as he cautiously approached the tiger.

"I was just thinking about you," the tiger said. "Actually, I feel kind of bad today. Worse than ever, in fact."

"Would you let me come in and examine you?" Dolittle asked. "I promise, I only want to help."

The tiger walked slowly to the cage door, reached up, and opened it with his paw. "Thanks, Doc," he said. "I feel so bad, I don't think I could go on tonight. Maybe you could fix me up before Oskar gets here or I'll be dead meat."

"Let's see!" Dolittle said. He walked confidently into the cage and closed the door behind himself. "Okay," he said. "Let me check out your vital signs first, do a few basic things, and we'll see what's going on."

He pulled the stethoscope from his doctor's bag and listened to the tiger's heart. "Lie down so I can check your eyes," he said to the tiger. He pulled his ophthalmoscope from his black bag and peered carefully into each huge eye.

"So Doc, what is it?" the tiger asked.

"I'm not sure," Dolittle said honestly. "But I'm going to call an expert on cats right now and find out what it all means. Okay?"

Dolittle pulled out his cell phone, called Fish, and reported his findings.

Fish replied, "The symptoms you describe could be caused by several different potential problems. The proper procedure would be to run a series of blood and urine tests." Fish spoke so loudly that the tiger could hear.

"I see," Dolittle replied. The tiger furiously shook his head.

Fish continued, "If the tests turn up negative, you may have to turn to the brain, which can be very, very tricky." Dolittle pressed the cell phone closer to his head and casually walked away from the tiger. "Uh-huh."

"There could be several problems, and all are difficult to find even with the latest technology," Fish continued. "There's only one sure way to determine the exact location of a head injury."

"What is that?" Dolittle asked.

Fish laughed, "Ask him where it hurts."

Dolittle took the phone from his ear. "Where does it hurt?" he asked the tiger.

"Right now behind my left eye. Other times it's my whole head," the tiger answered.

Dolittle put the phone back to his ear. "What if it is in the brain?" he asked Fish.

"Then there are usually only two options," Fish replied. "You either operate or put the tiger down."

"Well, I thank you for your help, Doctor," Dolittle said.

He shut the cell phone and turned to the tiger. "For now, the best thing is for you to rest. Don't even rehearse. I want to consult with one more doctor before we do anything, okay?"

"Whatever you say," the tiger said, stretching out on the floor. "Do you mind letting yourself out?"

Dolittle walked away, deeply concerned about the tiger's condition. He went over to the trainer's trailer. Oskar was at the door.

"Look," Dolittle said. "This is very serious. The tiger is sick and needs X rays, possibly brain surgery—"

Oskar laughed. "You're the one who needs brain surgery," he said. "Go away."

"But your tiger could die," Dolittle argued.

"Tigers die every day," Oskar said matter-of-factly. "It's called nature. Now get out of my circus!"

Dolittle headed for the parking lot.

Dolittle went back to the office. He walked past the alleyway near his building with his arms loaded with medical textbooks about large cats. Suddenly he heard a cry. A rat popped up from the Dumpster, crying, "Help me! You gotta help me! He's dead! He's lying in there dead! Please help me!"

Dolittle put down the textbooks and peered into the trash. Lying on his back moaning was one of the rats he'd met before.

"He's not dead," Dolittle told the first rat.

"I wish I was," the second rat moaned. Dolittle picked up his books and started to leave.

"No! No! Don't go! You gotta help him!" the first rat pleaded.

Dolittle turned around. "Why?" he asked.

" 'Cause . . . 'cause . . . you're *the man*!" the rat exclaimed.

"Oh, *now* I'm the man," Dolittle said. "Before, wasn't I the guy you wanted to make into a lamp?"

The first rat jumped up and down. "I was kidding! Can't you take a joke? Doctor, this is serious! I'm beggin' ya. Don't let him die! He's a rat, but he's still a good guy!"

Dolittle took a deep breath, put down the books, and walked to the Dumpster. Moments later he picked up the books and went up to his office. The place was packed. Dolittle sneaked in while Diane answered the telephone and spoke to patients waiting to be seen.

In one hand he carried the textbooks; in the other he held a plastic bag containing the two rats, who were creating a lot of noise and movement, making it look as if the bag had a life of its own. As Dolittle hurried toward an examination room, he ran into Mark Weller and Gene Reiss.

"John!" Reiss called.

"Not now," Dolittle answered.

Weller was angry. "Where the heck were you?"

"What?" Dolittle asked, looking confused.

"You missed the Calnet meeting!" Weller yelled.

Dolittle gasped. "Sorry! I had an emergency. Excuse me." He dashed into the exam room.

"Sure," Weller said with a look of concern. As he stood there, Diane called his name. "Dr. Weller, Mrs. Dolittle is on the phone. She wants to speak to you."

"I'll take the call in my office, Diane," Weller said, and walked down the hall.

Inside the examination room, Dolittle evaluated the sick rat who lay on the table.

"Does it hurt when I do this?" Dolittle asked.

"It ain't no day at the dump!" the rat shrieked.

"What did you eat?" Dolittle asked.

"I don't know. What kind of a restaurant is this?" the rat answered.

"It's not a restaurant," Dolittle said. "It's a medical building."

"That wasn't food I was eating?" the rat asked.

Dolittle shook his head.

"So what were those little crunchy . . . Oh no!" the rat cried, holding his stomach.

Down the hall, Weller was quietly talking to Lisa on the phone while Reiss stood next to him.

"He's been acting very weird here, too," Weller said to Lisa. "What's going on there?"

Lisa was sitting in her kitchen as she spoke to Weller. Facing her were three possums.

"You wouldn't believe it if I told you," she said.

"Maybe you should come over here now," Weller told her.

"Okay," she agreed. "I'll be right there."

Weller hung up and turned to Reiss. "I'm not going to let him blow this deal!"

Back in the exam room, Dolittle looked through the textbooks he'd brought in. The sick rat moaned constantly while his concerned friend watched and worried.

"If he died, I don't know what I'd do," the first rat said.

"You'd drag me outside and eat me," the sick rat groaned.

"Only out of respect," his friend answered.

Dolittle looked up from the books. "Would you guys shut up? I'm trying to find some answers here!"

Lisa arrived and went to Weller's office. She, Weller, and Reiss talked for a moment, then walked down the hall and stood outside the exam room Dolittle was using. They quietly pushed open the door. Lisa gasped as they saw Dolittle and a rat squeaking at each other. Lisa and the two doctors stood frozen in disbelief, unable to speak.

Dolittle looked up. "Oh, hi!" he said with a smile. "Lisa, what are you doing here? Are you all right?"

Lisa and the doctors stared at him, speechless.

Dolittle realized he had to explain about the rats. "One of them is sick," he said matter-of-factly. "He said he has severe abdominal cramps."

Lisa spoke first. "*He* said?"

Dolittle walked over to her. "I know it sounds impossible. I know it sounds crazy, but it's not. I'm not crazy," he said. He squeaked at the rat, who squeaked back.

Dolittle saw everyone's faces. "Why else would I be treating a rat if it wasn't an emergency?" he asked.

"Gene, Mark, feel for yourself. Lisa, don't look at me that way!"

The sick rat screamed and went rigid. Dolittle checked the artery in the rat's neck.

"There's no pulse!" Dolittle cried. He put his ear to the rat's mouth. "He's not breathing. He's gone into arrest." Dolittle started to give the rat CPR. He leaned down to listen again. "The heart has to be somewhere near here," he said. He turned to Reiss. "Should I shock him?"

Dolittle furiously tried to pump on the rat's little heart. Lisa approached him and gently put her arm on his. Why was her husband talking to animals? Was he going crazy?

"Honey," Lisa said softly.

"Not now!" Dolittle said.

"John!" Lisa shouted.

"Lisa! I'm trying to save a life here!" he yelled at her.

Suddenly a loud noise broke the tension. *"Burp!"* The rat came to life. "I'm hungry!" the formerly sick rat said, burping loudly again.

Dolittle looked at his wife, almost embarrassed. "False alarm," he smiled. "It must have been gas."

olittle sat in the passenger seat beside Lisa. She drove up a long driveway. At the end of the driveway, behind a locked fence, stood a huge mansion in the midst of green rolling hills.

"It's really like a retreat or rest home, honey," Lisa said, watching her husband out of the corner of her eye. Dolittle sat back, enjoying the pretty scenery and the comfortable ride. He thought they were going to a fancy bed-and-breakfast for a few days' rest and would have a wonderful time. Antique furnishings, elegant meals, relaxing four o'clock teas. This would be great!

Lisa stopped at the gatehouse and spoke quietly to the guard, who pressed a button that opened the gate. The house was magnificent, but something about it seemed odd. Suddenly John realized this was *not* a vacation trip.

"Come on, honey," Lisa coaxed. "Scott is waiting for us. A little rest and you'll be good as new." They entered the building. Patients in pajamas were being led around by attendants. Dr. Scott Sherman waited at the desk.

He came over to them. "John, don't think of this as an insane asylum," he said, pulling Dolittle aside. "It's just a place for—"

"People who talk to animals," Dolittle said.

"Hey," Sherman laughed, "*anyone* can talk to animals."

"Yeah, but I *understand* them," Dolittle pointed out.

"Maybe you should just concentrate on getting better," Sherman suggested.

"See, that's the thing," Dolittle said, looking his friend straight in the eye. "I really don't think I'm sick."

"Rest," Sherman said, preparing to go back to his office. "Lots and lots of rest and you'll be better."

Dolittle and Lisa walked arm in arm out to the rambling front porch and sat on a wicker sofa.

Lisa's eyes overflowed with tears.

"Hey, hey," Dolittle said, pulling her close to him. "It's going to be fine."

"I know, I know," she said hesitantly.

"How are the girls?"

"Fine. Charisse thinks this is her fault—that she drove you over the edge with Paprika, so now she's back to being Charisse. And Maya . . ." Lisa hesitated again.

"What?"

"Well, I think it would really upset her to see you here. She's only got two weeks at camp. And by then, Scott thinks you might be able to come home—"

"Two weeks?" Dolittle repeated. "I'm not staying here two weeks. No way."

"Scott is recommending you stay a minimum of ten days," Lisa explained.

"Forget it," he said.

"Look, John," she said, trying to pull herself together. "You said you could talk to animals. That simply does not make sense."

"I know that," he said. "But I'm telling you that it's true and I'm asking you to believe me." Just then a pigeon flew onto a small table next to the sofa.

"Not now," Dolittle said to the bird. The bird flew away. Dolittle looked at Lisa. She had tears in her eyes.

She hugged him tightly. "I'll call you tomorrow," she said. She kissed his cheek and walked off the porch and over to the car. Dolittle waved as she drove out the gate, which locked behind her.

While Dolittle was settling in at the clinic, Mark Weller was working in his office. Diane knocked on the door.

"Dr. Weller, Mr. Calloway from Calnet is here to see you," she said, sounding distressed.

"Tell him I'll be right—" before Weller could finish, Calloway stormed into the office with his assistant, Carson.

Weller sat up. "Mr. Calloway, what a nice surprise. I just got off the phone with John Dolittle from— uh—Bangladesh."

"Cut the baloney, Weller," Calloway said. "Word is Dolittle's taking a little rest at a clinic."

"No, no, not true," Weller assured him.

Calloway slammed his fist on Weller's desk. "It better not be. No Dolittle, no deal. Got it?"

"What if John was there in spirit?" Weller asked hesitantly.

Carson cut him off. "We need all three of you. For publicity."

"He'll be there tomorrow night, Mr. Calloway, if I have to bring him back from Bangladesh myself," Weller said. Calloway and Carson left.

Weller immediately drove out to the clinic to see Dolittle. They sat in the rec room. Weller was sweating nervously, but Dolittle looked relaxed, sorting his mail and looking through files.

"What's wrong with *you*?" Dolittle asked.

"I'm worried, John," Weller admitted.

"Don't worry, I'll be fine. Just fine," Dolittle said.

"It's not you I'm worried about. It's Gene. He's not taking this well," Weller said.

Not believing Weller's story, Dolittle shook his head in concern. "Huh? *Really?*"

"He's torn up about this," Weller continued.

Dolittle tilted his head. "That's funny. I talked to him last night. He sounded just fine. Mark, don't horse around with me. You're *not* worried about Gene. You're worried about Calnet and the deal!"

"Okay, okay, I admit it," Weller said. "I want the money. Is that so wrong? John, look, I don't think you can talk to animals, okay? But even if you think you can, what is the point? Who cares? They're animals, for Christ's sake. We *wear* them!" He was shouting now. "Calloway called. If you're not back by Friday, the deal's off. I talked to your doctor, Sherman, here. You could probably convince him to get you out if you just stopped barking or cooing for a day. Think about it so we can get this deal done!" Weller stormed out of the clinic.

The next morning, Dolittle went along with other patients for coffee and donuts in the rec room. Wearing his clinic pajamas, unshaven and red-eyed, he already resembled his fellow patients.

He spent the day watching TV, sleeping, and eating in the main dining room. He didn't shower or shave or change out of the pajamas all day. That night he gathered in the rec room with several patients. They sat at a card table, involved in a heated discussion.

Suddenly Dolittle heard a familiar voice coming from outside the window. "Psst! Doc. Out here!" He walked to the window and spotted Lucky looking up at him.

Dolittle opened the window. "How'd you get here?" he asked the dog.

"You look ridiculous!" Lucky said, shaking his head in disgust.

"What are you doing here?" Dolittle demanded of Lucky.

The dog paced back and forth. "You know, you're unbelievable. I cross three freeways to come rescue you and all I get is 'What are you doing here?' "

"Rescue?" Dolittle looked bewildered. "This isn't a prison, it's a clinic," he protested.

"Look," Lucky said. "The tiger's in bad shape."

"So am I," Dolittle said, looking at his reflection in a mirror on the wall.

"You're fine," Lucky reassured him.

Dolittle shook his head. "I *was* fine. I've had a very good life so far. I have a terrific family, a very good job, and a deal for a lot of money waiting for me. And I'm going to throw it all away just to save a tiger? Everyone must be right. I am crazy!" Dolittle laughed.

"Is it crazy to want to save a tiger's life?" Lucky asked.

"Tigers die every day! It's called nature," Dolittle said, echoing Oskar the trainer.

Lucky stared hard at Dolittle. "Let me tell you about nature," Lucky said. "I'm a dog, and I act like a dog. I don't want to try to be anybody else. And you—you're a doctor with a special gift, a God-given gift. You can talk to animals!"

"No!" Dolittle protested.

"That's who you are!" Lucky said.

"Wrong!" Dolittle argued, a bit more weakly.

"Stop lying to yourself, Doc," Lucky persisted. "You have a gift. And it could save the tiger's life."

"Get out of here," Dolittle said, starting to turn from the window.

"Fine," Lucky angrily answered. He started to walk away.

"Beat it!" Dolittle called after him.

"With pleasure!" Lucky called back.

"Go!" Dolittle shouted.

Lucky turned around. "What does it look like I'm doing?"

"And stay away! All of you!" Dolittle said. Tears came to his eyes. He took a rock from the window ledge and threw it. Nearby birds flew away. Dolittle turned, closed the window tightly, and went back to the table.

The clinic was taking its toll on Dolittle. By the next morning he looked exactly like all the other patients. Again he shuffled into the rec room wearing pajamas and a bathrobe. As he started to pour himself a cup of coffee, a pigeon landed on the ledge of an opened window. The pigeon cooed.

"Go away!" Dolittle said.

The pigeon walked up and down the window ledge.

"Go!" Dolittle repeated, but the pigeon didn't seem to understand and cooed again.

"Hey, you're not talking, you're cooing," Dolittle said, staring at the pigeon. The pigeon stared back and cooed again.

"Watch it!" Dolittle said in a scary pigeon voice. "Owl's coming to get you!"

The pigeon didn't move.

"You didn't understand me!" Dolittle said in amazement. He turned to the other patients, who stood around looking at him as he made bird sounds. "He just cooed! He didn't understand me. I don't talk to animals anymore!"

"Gee, I'm sorry," one patient said.

Dolittle put down his coffee and ran to find Scott Sherman. He knocked on Sherman's office door and walked in.

"Scott! I'm cured!" he said, running around the desk and hugging the amazed physician. "I just tried to talk to a pigeon and he didn't understand me. This place is a house of miracles! Can I go now?"

Sherman took a deep breath and told Dolittle to sit down. "Look," Sherman said. "I can't let you go. It's too soon!"

Dolittle sat forward, excited. "I'm telling you, it's like a fever that broke. I feel fine. Great! *Terrific!*"

"John, what do you tell *your* patients when they say that?" Sherman asked. "You say, 'Don't overdo it, take it easy for a few more days,' right?"

"I want to go home," Dolittle said. He spotted a cat putting his head around the door and meowing.

"Sherm, what do you hear?" Dolittle asked.

"A cat." Sherman answered.

"Me too!" Dolittle said, grinning.

"I hear it *meowing*," Sherman said pointedly.

"Me too!" Dolittle laughed. "C'mon, what's the big deal?"

Sherman threw up his hands in frustration. "*All right*. But you have to understand something. I can always find an excuse for admitting you once. But if you have to be *readmitted*, they could suspend your medical license for a very, very long time."

"I assure you, that won't be a problem, Sherm," Dolittle said. He shook the other doctor's hand and patted him on the back. "Thanks, you're a real friend."

A short time later, Dolittle was home. He opened the front door and saw Maya examining her large egg.

She turned, surprised to see him.

"Honey, hi!" he said.

Maya smiled. "Daddy, you're home! I thought you were in the hospital! Are you okay?" she asked, running into his arms.

"Fine," Dolittle said, giving her a big hug. "I didn't belong there. And I thought you were still at camp."

"John?" Lisa called from the kitchen, hearing his voice.

"I didn't belong there, either, Daddy," Maya said.

Lisa and Charisse came running into the hallway.

"Daddy's home! Daddy's home!" Charisse shouted. Lisa smiled, walked to Dolittle, and welcomed him with a kiss.

Lucky sat on the floor in the corner. He looked at Dolittle but did not approach him.

After a quick breakfast with the girls and Lisa, John changed into a suit, picked up his papers and medical bag, and went to the office. As he walked in, Diane was on the phone. She looked up, shocked to see him. He waved and smiled.

Dolittle walked into the back and straight to his office. He buzzed Diane. "Diane, could you please call Radiology and get me the X rays for Mr. Galvin?" he said, sounding like his old self.

"Yes, Doctor. Certainly," she said.

"And one more thing," he said as he looked over his schedule. "Could you try to switch Mrs. Rivers to three o'clock?"

"Yes, Doctor," Diane said."

After reviewing his charts, Dolittle went from his office to the conference room, where Weller and Reiss sat looking at papers. Dolittle walked in and took his white coat out of the closet.

"Gene, can you look at your schedule and try to make room for a three-fifteen consult?" he said, heading for the door again.

"Sure," Reiss said, still looking at his papers.

"Mark, any of the tests back on Mr. Freeman?" Dolittle asked.

"Due in this afternoon," Weller said.

"Good," Dolittle said. He pointed to the open window. A pigeon sat on the ledge. "And have someone call Maintenance and tell them either to put in permanent screens or set some traps. This is a doctor's office!" he said. He closed the door behind him.

Weller looked up and stared at Reiss. "He's back!"

That night the family dressed up for the press conference announcing the doctors' deal with Calnet. In suits and ties, Dolittle's father, Archer, and Dolittle crawled on the floor with Maya, looking for Rodney, the guinea pig.

"Here, Rodney, here, boy . . . Keep looking, Grandpa," Maya said. "He usually leaves a trail."

"Oh, great!" Archer scowled. He stood and continued looking on his feet rather than on the knees of his good suit.

"Can't you call him, Dad?" Maya asked. "He'll answer *you*!"

Her father ignored that comment and stood. "We'll find him after the press conference. We've got to get going," he said, dusting off his knees.

"Daddy, I know you can talk to animals," Maya said, looking at him seriously.

Dolittle gave her a look that was equally serious. "Maya, people can't talk to animals. And animals can't talk to people. And that's that. Now, just get ready to go. I don't want to be late." He walked out of her room.

Maya turned to her grandfather. "Sometimes I don't think Daddy likes me very much," she said.

Her grandfather pulled her onto his lap and gave her a hug. "Oh, honey, he loves you very much."

"I know he loves me," the sharp-eyed nine-year-old said. "But I don't think he *likes* me. I want him to. I'm going to try to do things his way, Grandpa. I want to make friends and do things Daddy likes to do. Grandpa, can I tell you a secret?"

"Course you can."

"When Mom called and told me what happened with Daddy, I wasn't scared. I was happy! 'Cause I believed he could talk to animals. I wanted Dad to be weird like me! Is that weird?" Maya asked.

"No, no, it's not," Archer said, kissing her cheek.

Suddenly she hopped off his lap. "Wait—I thought I just saw Rodney!"

Maya crawled under her desk. Archer looked toward the door, where his son had been standing, listening to Maya. Dolittle looked back at his father.

91

Dolittle drove everyone to the office for the press conference announcing the deal with Calnet.

Pulling the car up to the front door, he waited as Lisa, Archer, and Charisse got out. "Maya," he said as she started to hop down, "why don't you come with me to park? We'll meet them inside."

"Sure, Daddy," she said, climbing into the front seat, holding Rodney.

"Okay, but hurry," Lisa called. Dolittle drove across the parking lot. He pulled into his spot and turned off the ignition. Maya started to get out.

"Maya, wait," Dolittle called. She turned around. "I just want you to know your egg isn't a stupid experiment. I think it's cool!"

"You do?" His daughter beamed.

Dolittle nodded. "Yeah, I do. You've got a lot of curiosity and good ideas. That's what makes you special."

"You mean *weird*," she said, making a face.

"No. I mean *special*," he repeated. "But let me tell you something: There's nothing wrong with weird. A lot of great people in history were considered weird. *Super*-weird . . ."

"Like who?" She smiled.

"*Who?* Well, like Albert Einstein with his crazy hair," Dolittle said. "And Muhammad Ali talked crazy and acted crazy but was the greatest boxer ever.

Rosa Parks thought she could sit where she wanted to, and she made it possible for other people to do just that. Joan of Arc heard voices—"

"Like you, Dad?" Maya asked.

"I guess like me," he said, flashing a big smile. "But remember, no matter what happens to me—be who *you* are, love who you are, because I sure do." He reached over, and they hugged.

Dolittle smiled. "Now, you go on inside and tell the others I'll be back as soon as I can."

"Okay, Daddy," Maya said, getting out of the car. "Hey, Dad," she called back to him. "I think you're a great person!" She ran inside.

Dolittle drove off. As he stopped at a traffic light he heard the sound of crying from the rear of the car.

"That was beautiful, man," Lucky cried, leaning over the backseat.

Dolittle jerked around. "*You*? What are you doing here?"

"I knew you'd come around," Lucky said, choking back his tears.

"How come we can talk again?" Dolittle asked. "I mean, I thought I stopped!"

Lucky explained, "You never stopped, Doc. You just buried it for a while, kinda like a bone in the backyard. Hey. Nice analogy, huh? You can bury it, cover it with dirt, but it's still there, waiting for you when you really need it—"

"Speak English!" Dolittle demanded.

Lucky sat up on the seat. "You care, Doc. And when you really care, anything is possible." He leaned forward. "It's the best part of you, so stop fighting it, will ya?"

Dolittle sighed deeply. "All right," he said finally.

"Good, now where're we going?" Lucky asked.

"To do something crazy. Hang on," Dolittle instructed. He zoomed the car around a corner and headed to the circus grounds.

Dolittle went straight to the tiger's cage. The animal was asleep on the floor.

"Hey," Dolittle whispered.

"Jeez!" the tiger said, jumping to his feet. "Stop sneaking up on me!"

"Shhh!" Dolittle said, his finger to his lips. "Listen, you're sick and you need help. I want to do some tests."

The tiger paced back and forth, trying to ignore him. "I'm fine."

A voice spoke up. "He hasn't been out of his cage for a week." Dolittle turned to see the orangutan in his cage, standing at the bars.

The tiger shrugged. "It's nothing."

"Let me tell you something," Dolittle said, starting to raise his voice. "It's time to swallow your pride. You're sick, and you're getting sicker. And you know as well as I do what they do with sick animals around here."

The tiger thought for a moment as he looked at Dolittle. "Okay, I guess you're right," he said. Dolittle opened the cage door and the tiger followed him. As they walked past the elephant cage, the elephant called, "Take good care of him, Doc. He's our star!"

The tiger and Dolittle sneaked past the cages and off the grounds toward the parking lot.

"Be stealthy, catlike," Dolittle whispered as he suddenly spotted a security guard.

"Hey," the tiger said, smiling. "That's Jerry! He's a fan of mine!"

"Keep it down!" Dolittle said. But the tiger didn't listen. "Hey, Jerry! Hey there!" he growled toward the guard, attracting the guard's attention and his bright flashlight.

"Hey, what the . . . ," Jerry said. He watched as the tiger followed Dolittle to the car in the parking lot. "Code three, code three!" Jerry said into his walkie-talkie, and then chased after them.

"A fan, huh? Is that why he's calling for backup?" Dolittle yelled at the tiger. "Exit stage right, now!" he said. He opened the back door of the car. The tiger jumped in. Dr. Dolittle slammed the door shut and leaped into the driver's seat.

Lucky sat up and faced the tiger. "Stop looking at me like I'm a side dish," he said.

"Don't flatter yourself," the tiger growled. "You're barely a mouthful."

"Quiet, you two!" Dolittle said. He spotted several security guards running around with flashlights.

Jerry the guard saw the tiger in the rear of the car and shined his light at them. "Hey! Halt! Stop right there!" he shouted. Dolittle picked up speed, leaving the guard in the dust.

Back at the medical building, concern mounted. Dolittle was late for the big Calnet press conference. The Calnet logo hung on the wall in the office waiting room, which was jammed with reporters, video crews, and a bank of microphones. Weller and Reiss were sweating. Calloway looked at his watch.

"You said he'd be here," Calloway said, walking over to Weller.

Weller tried to look calm. "Of course he will. Mr. Calloway, if I may speak for my partners, I know how excited they are to be a part of your organization," he said.

"Weller," Calloway shot back angrily, "listen up and listen good. The only reason we're making this deal is for your partners. You're unfortunately part of the package. Consider yourself very expensive bubble wrap." He turned on his heel and walked away.

In another corner Dolittle's father, Archer, stood worrying. Lisa came over and stood next to him. "I called home," she whispered. "No answer."

"He'll turn up," Archer assured her. "Don't worry."

"Charisse!" Lisa called to her daughter. "Where's your sister?"

Charisse pointed to Maya, who was wearing a fancy dress and crawling on the floor under a table. "Rodney escaped again," Charisse said.

Maya called Rodney, but he was hiding under the long tablecloth at the refreshment table.

"I love parties," Rodney said. He sniffed at a nut that had fallen to the floor. "A macadamia! I've died and gone to heaven," he said, picking up the nut and stuffing it in his mouth. Maya continued going from table to table, still unable to find him.

Dolittle parked in his spot and got out of the car, followed by Lucky and the tiger.

Dolittle turned to Lucky. "Keep an eye out."

The doctor pointed toward the entrance. The tiger hesitated. "C'mon!" Dolittle said. "Hurry!" The tiger followed him in.

Upstairs in the office, everyone was growing tense. Maya continued crawling around, looking for Rodney. From under the table she heard Weller, Reiss, and Calloway's assistant, Carson, talking.

"You don't understand," Reiss said, sounding

agitated. "I like having close relationships with my patients. That's more important to me than having this deal and the money."

Weller laughed. "You'll get over it."

Reiss shook his head and walked away, exiting through swinging doors to the laboratory.

"He'd better get with the program, Mark," Carson said, pointing after Reiss.

Weller waved a hand. "He will. Don't worry about it."

Weller and Carson strolled by the swinging lab doors. As they passed, one of the doors swung open, whacking Weller in the face.

"Ow! Ow!" he shouted. He grabbed his nose, howling in pain.

Reiss walked out from the opposite side.

"Mark! Oh, God! I'm so sorry! I didn't see you, honest!" Reiss said, stifling a laugh as his friend held a handkerchief to his bloody nose.

"It's broken!" Weller shouted. "You broke my nose!"

"What a terrible, terrible accident," Reiss said, shaking his head.

Calloway came bustling over. "What's happened now?" he asked, exasperated.

"Mark's nose might be broken," Reiss said. Pretending to examine it, he tweaked it hard.

"Owww!" Weller yelled.

"Definitely broken," Reiss said with a straight face.

"Do something!" Calloway said angrily, pushing them all in a corner away from the reporters.

"I'll take him down to X ray," Reiss said.

"All right. But hurry. We can't stall much longer," Calloway said. "And where in God's name is Dolittle?"

"He's on his way, I'm sure," Lisa said, taking Calloway by the arm and leading him to the refreshments table for a drink.

Reiss led Weller out of the waiting room.

"Oh, God, if it's broken, I want you to set it," Weller said to him.

"Of course," Reiss said. "But to do that, I may have to rebreak it. You know, to get it right."

Weller groaned. As they walked one way down the hall toward X ray, Dolittle and the tiger were walking there from the opposite direction.

The tiger walked very slowly, looking around anxiously. "This is where you work?" he asked.

"Yeah," Dolittle said, trying to hurry him along.

"Where do the people sit to watch you?" the tiger asked as they entered the X-ray room.

"What are you talking about?" Dolittle said. "This is a private practice."

"No crowds? No applause?" the tiger asked, looking surprised. "What's the point?"

Just as they entered, Weller and Reiss approached.

Mark held his handkerchief to his nose, complaining, "This really hurts. I can hardly breathe."

"It should; your septum is crushed," Reiss said. "Breathe through your mouth. You'll be fine."

As they walked into the outer X-ray room, Dolittle walked out of the X-ray control room inside it.

"John!" Reiss shouted.

"Oh, hey, fellas," Dolittle said awkwardly.

"Dolittle!" Weller said angrily, almost forgetting to keep his nose covered.

Dolittle smiled at him. "Hey, what happened to you?"

"I walked into a door," Weller said lamely.

"Actually," Reiss explained, mouthing the words, "I opened it on him."

Weller gawked at Dolittle. "John, what are you doing down here? You're supposed to be at the press conference. Calloway is ready to split a gut!"

"Well, uh . . . look, I have someone with me," Dolittle said apologetically. The tiger sauntered in from the control room.

"Jesus!" Weller said, dropping his handkerchief and jumping back toward the door.

"It's okay, fellas. Really it is." Dolittle tried to calm them.

"It's a—a—" Reiss stammered.

"A *tiger*!" Weller screamed. The tiger roared.

Weller and Reiss jumped, totally terrified, and ran out the door.

"That hurt," the tiger said. "I was just being friendly."

"Do me a favor, will you?" Dolittle said. "Don't speak."

"I can't help it," the tiger said. "People just get excited when they see me."

Weller and Reiss raced toward the elevator. When the elevator door opened, Carson stood there, looking at them angrily. "Mr. Calloway's getting cold feet," he said. "This whole deal could go down the tubes any minute, you guys."

Weller quickly regained his composure. "No, no, no, no," he laughed. "No problems, really. "We found Dolittle. Tell Mr. Calloway we'll all be up in five minutes. Five little minutes." He pushed Carson back into the elevator and pressed the Up arrow.

The elevator door closed. Weller turned to Reiss. "All right," Weller said, thinking fast. "This is what we do. Let's tell John we'll help him with that animal *after* we sign. Then we go up, we sign, then we have John put back in the loony bin where he belongs. That way we'll have our money and we'll be rid of that crazy Dolittle. It's a perfect plan for—"

Reiss looked Weller straight in the eye, gave him a

mean look, and punched him in the nose, hard. Weller fell to the floor, out cold.

"Told you I might have to rebreak it," Reiss said. He went back to the X-ray room to find Dolittle.

hree policemen encircled Oskar the trainer, trying to get information from him on the tiger getaway.

"I tell you, it was that crazy man. I think the clowns sent him to make jokes. He told me the tiger was sick," Oskar said. "That tiger is just old. Get rid of him. There is always another tiger. I saw that crazy man drive away. He had letters on the back of his car. *S, A,* uh, . . ."

Finally one policeman thrust a pen and notepad into Oskar's hand. "Just write it down, buddy, so we can go after the big cat."

"Yes! Good idea!" Oskar said. "I'll write it down!"

As he wrote down the license plate number, the policeman called it in to headquarters on his radio.

Two pigeons watched and listened from a tree above the circus grounds.

"Do something," the female pigeon urged her mate.

"The heart of a hawk, the heart of a hawk," the male pigeon repeated to himself, feeling the words giving him courage. He flew off over San Francisco. When he spotted the police horse on the streets below, the pigeon landed on a nearby trash can.

"Oh, oh, oh," the pigeon panted, trying to catch his breath.

The horse was not wearing his glasses, and all he could see was a blurry image of a bird on the trash can. "I don't have my glasses," he said. "Identify yourself."

"I'm a very, very out-of-shape hawk," the pigeon said, beginning to breathe normally.

"I can't see very much. But you ain't no hawk," the horse said.

"Look, never mind me," the pigeon said. "Doc's trying to save the tiger, but the cops want to stop him."

The policeman sitting on the horse's back received a message over his radio. The horse heard him say, "Roger. Four one nine is proceeding to the twenty." He kicked the horse's side. "Let's go!" he said.

The horse didn't move.

104

"I said let's go!" the policeman repeated, kicking him harder. "Hiyaaaah!"

The horse just whinnied, then sat on the ground. The officer jumped up and desperately started shouting at the horse, who sat there ignoring him.

Back in the X-ray control room, Dolittle and Reiss were looking at pictures of the tiger's head. Weller lay unconscious, with an ice pack on his nose, on a gurney next to the tiger's gurney. (Gurneys are rolling tables patients are moved on when they go in for operations.)

"So what are you going to do?" Reiss asked Dolittle.

"It looks like the pineal gland is calcified," Dolittle said, looking from one X ray to the next.

"We've got to get him into the O.R. right now. It's the only chance he's got."

Reiss stared at Dolittle. "John, you can't do brain surgery on a tiger, especially when you don't know what you're looking for. How are you going to find it?"

Dolittle stared back at Reiss. "He's going to tell me where it is. He'll feel numbness if I'm too close to the motor strip. Gene, I need your help."

"Even if I say yes, to get the tiger to the operating room you'd have to wheel him right through the middle of the press conference that's going on out there." Reiss thought for a moment, then smiled. He suddenly realized that this would kill the Calnet deal, and he'd be able to keep the office the way he liked it.

Outside, the plight of Dr. Dolittle was being broadcast throughout the animal world of San Francisco. Lucky ran up and down streets like a canine Paul Revere, calling out, "Doc's in trouble! Doc's in trouble!" Word spread quickly throughout the city.

Inside the waiting room, everyone was getting restless, waiting for the missing doctors. Maya was still looking for Rodney. She passed a reporter and cameraman as she crawled along the edge of the room.

"God, I hate these slow news days," the reporter said. "This is so boring. And there's a great game on tonight too."

Maya crawled out the waiting room door just as Dolittle and Gene pushed a gurney off the elevator. The gurney carried a sheet-covered form. From down on the floor, Maya saw the tiger's legs. She watched as Dolittle quickly adjusted the sheet to hide the tiger.

Dolittle and Reiss pushed the gurney into the waiting room. "Coming through," Dolittle called. "Please clear a path. We have an emergency." He and Reiss pushed the "patient" along until they were stopped by Calloway and Lisa, who blocked their path.

"There you are," Calloway said. "Let's do this deal already."

"Mark's nose is broken," Dolittle explained. "We're going to have to set it immediately."

"His nose can wait," Calloway said. He called to the reporters and camerapeople. "Weller's nose can wait," he repeated. "Come on, partners. We're announcing right now."

As Calloway led Reiss and Dolittle to the podium in the middle of the room, Lisa took her husband's arm.

"Where were you? What happened?" she asked.

"I'll explain later," he said, flashing a broad grin.

Maya walked over to her sister and tugged on her arm.

"What?" Charisse said, turning.

"C'mere," Maya said, pulling her away.

Dolittle and Reiss each took a position next to Calloway. They both looked toward the gurney with worried glances. Would the tiger remain asleep?

Calloway stood at the microphone. "Thank you all for coming," he said. "As you all know, we at Calnet strive to be at the forefront of the medical business world. That's why we're pleased to announce our deal with one of San Francisco's premier medical practices. . . ."

The crowd faced Calloway as he droned on and on. Behind them Rodney had jumped onto the buffet table and was checking out the food. He spotted a bowl of snacks. "Oh my God, I love party mix!" He sat down and started munching away. Also behind the backs of the crowd, the tiger peered out from under the sheet and spotted Rodney on the table.

"Oh my," the tiger said to himself. "Live prey!" He slid onto the floor with the sheet tangled around him and attached to the gurney. The tiger started toward Rodney, who kept munching on the junk food.

Calloway continued his talk. "Doctors Dolittle, Weller, and Reiss have built a thriving office practice, and—"

Dolittle looked to his side. He gasped when he saw the gurney moving as the tiger pulled the sheet along with him toward the food table, where Rodney was eating.

Other people began to notice.

Calloway finished his speech. "So it is with the greatest pleasure that I welcome to the Calnet family Doctors Dolittle, Weller, and Reiss." He led the room in applause.

Maya and Charisse discreetly leaned down next to the gurney and saw the tiger's feet. Dolittle waved to the girls to get away from the table. Lisa looked at Dolittle and the girls. She knew something was going on.

Rodney turned and spotted the gurney, pulled by the tiger, coming toward him. He stared and said to himself, "What the . . ."

The gurney stopped, but the tiger kept going. The roomful of people saw the tiger approach the table.

Maya spotted Rodney and screamed. Dolittle jumped across the room and grabbed the guinea pig just as the tiger reached him and leaped to the table. Everyone scattered, screaming and running, terrified of the tiger. The tiger dropped from the table to the floor. Dolittle rushed to where the tiger was lying.

"Sorry, Doc, I guess my instinct just took over," the tiger apologized. Dolittle felt the tiger's pulse.

"I feel weak, and my head's killing me," the tiger said.

The camera crews were taping madly. The reporters went to live television, giving an exclusive on what was happening.

Dr. Dolittle shouted to the crowd to be calm. "Don't worry, everyone. He's not going to hurt anyone. He's very sick."

Charrisse went to her father. She knelt next to the tiger and patted his fur. "Daddy, were you talking to this tiger?"

"Yes, yes, I was." Dolittle smiled weakly. "He won't hurt anyone."

Calloway remained at the microphone, sputtering as he spoke. "Now, I'm sure there's some rational explanation for this," he said.

Dolittle stood up. "Yes, sir, there is. The rational explanation is that I can talk to animals. And right now this tiger is telling me he's about to die." The cameras were all focused on Dolittle.

"That's preposterous, John," Calloway shouted. "You're joking. This must be some kind of joke."

Dolittle spoke up. "No. You see, that's the difference between you and me, Mr. Calloway. I believe in miracles and you don't."

People in the room cheered and applauded. Archer Dolittle looked at his son with tears in his eyes. "Go do what you need to do," he said to his son.

"Thanks, Dad," Dolittle said. He turned to the tiger. "C'mon. Can you make it on your feet?"

"You kidding?" The tiger smiled. "I've got an audience. Step, turn, look . . . growl."

As he growled, people jumped back, holding on to each other, frightened but enthralled.

Dolittle led the tiger across the room and through the doors into the operating room.

Inside the operating room, the tiger stretched out on a sheet-covered table. Bright lights focused on him as Reiss and Dolittle pushed in trays of instruments. A bank of machines stood nearby. Dolittle called to the tiger. "Be right back," he said. "We're going to scrub."

Reiss and Dolittle carefully washed their hands. The doctors were dressed in green operating suits, with green caps on their heads.

"Okay," Dolittle said as he leaned close to the tiger. "Now, we're going to do this as a team. I need you to stay awake and tell me when you feel any numbness in your paws, or down your right side. Can you do that for me?"

"Doc," the tiger said. "You should know—that thing about cats having nine lives?"

Dolittle nodded.

"Myth," the tiger said. "Not true."

"You mean I have to get this operation right the first time?" Dolittle said, pretending to be surprised.

The tiger laughed. "Yup. One life, Doc. And I'm not done with it yet," he said.

"I know," Dolittle said, putting on the operating light. "Here we go. Spotlight, center stage."

"We're on!" the tiger said, relaxing under the bright glare.

Outside the operating room, Archer, Maya, Charisse, and Lisa stood waiting. "He can't do this," Lisa said, sounding hysterical. "He thinks he can talk to the animals again!"

Archer put his arm around his daughter-in-law and turned her to face him. "He *can*, Lisa," he said.

She looked at him in disbelief.

"He really can," Archer continued. "It started when John was a little kid. I didn't know what to do. . . ."

"What are you saying?" Lisa said softly, over-whelmed. Archer and Lisa moved to a group of chairs in the corridor near a nurse's desk and had a talk.

Inside the operating room, Dolittle explained each step to the tiger as he proceeded, hoping to keep the big cat relaxed.

"This won't hurt," Dolittle said. "It's just gonna

feel like a beesting." He gently gave the tiger an injection with a small needle. The tiger jumped.

Reiss and Dolittle stood on either side of the tiger's head. "You sure you know how to do brain surgery on a tiger?" Reiss asked.

"I'm not sure of anything anymore," Dolittle admitted.

"Whatever happens, Doc," the tiger said, "I feel blessed for having met you."

"No," Dolittle said. "I'm the one who's been blessed."

The tiger closed his eyes. "Thanks," he said. "Let the show begin."

As the operation got under way, police cars gathered outside the medical building, lights flashing. But the police were unable to get into the building. Hundreds of animals of all kinds, including goats, sheep, horses, rabbits, dogs, cats, and raccoons, were blocking the entrance.

At the front of the crowd, Lucky the dog paced back and forth, leading the animals in a cheer: "One, two, three, four, you ain't gettin' through this door!"

The baffled police just stared at the barking dog and the incredible situation, with the animals in complete control. The male pigeon perched on a lower building ledge along with dozens of other birds. They looked down with pride, caught up in the emotion of the moment.

Inside the operating room, Reiss and Dolittle were working on the tiger. "Feel anything now?" Dolittle asked the tiger.

"No, just the same old pain," the tiger replied.

"Now? What about now? Any numbness?" Dolittle asked.

"I—I can't," the tiger stammered shakily. "I don't know." He started to raise his head from the table.

"Don't let him do that!" Reiss told Dolittle.

Dolittle patted the tiger's brow. "Shhh," he said gently. "It's all right. It's all right. Just relax and try to listen to my voice. I won't let you go."

A huge tear dripped from the tiger's eye. "I'm scared," he said.

Dolittle spoke to him, and the tiger gradually quieted down. The doctor looked up for a moment and saw Lisa standing in the operating room.

"What is he saying?" she asked.

He looked at her and took a deep breath. She believed him! She believed he could talk to animals! "He's just scared," he explained.

Lisa looked at the tiger and gently took his paw in her hand. The tiger seemed to calm even more at her touch. Lisa and Dolittle looked at each other and smiled.

"The brain is bulging here," Reiss said, sounding upset.

"Take it slow," Dolittle said to his partner. "Hang in there," he said to the tiger.

Dozens of animals were watching the operation through the window as the surgeons cut into the tiger's head, hoping to rid the animal of his pain.

"A little more," Dolittle said. "A little more. Now!" he shouted.

"Hurry!" Reiss said. "He's going into shock!"

The tiger went rigid; his eyes rolled back; his paw dropped from Lisa's hand. Dolittle rapidly inserted a tube into the tiger. The huge patient seemed to be dying.

"Hang on," Dolittle called to the tiger. "The show's not over. Come on. . . . Almost there . . . Hold on. . . ."

The animals watching in the window were still as stones. Lisa and Reiss looked panicked.

"Got it!" Dolittle finally shouted. Suddenly the tiger opened his eyes and raised his paw. *"There,"* he said weakly. "That's it."

"All right!" Dolittle cried. "He's back!"

"Blood pressure stabilizing," Reiss reported, letting out a sigh of relief.

The tiger took his paw and put it on Dolittle's shoulder. "It's gone, Doc. The pain's gone," he said.

Dolittle smiled. He looked up to see the rest of his family standing along the back of the operating room. He smiled and looked at his father, who was holding Charisse and Maya. The girls were beaming. Archer nodded his approval. Dolittle met Lisa's eyes. She smiled proudly and gave him a thumbs-up.

Dolittle and Reiss closed the incision as everyone watched. Sitting in the safety of Maya's pocket, the only one to speak was Rodney. "You the man! Doc! Yes! You the *man*!"

Outside the windows, the animals excitedly jumped up and down, waving to the doctor and calling the good news to those too short to see. Dolittle shut off the bright lights as he and Reiss completed the surgery. Together they heard applause from the crowd of humans and animals.

"Thank you," the tiger said softly.

"Rest easy now," Dolittle said. "We did it. You'll be back in the ring in no time."

Calloway and Weller stood in the hallway outside the operating room.

"Dolittle's a lunatic with a history of mental illness. He's outta here," Weller said, holding his broken nose. "We don't need him for—"

Calloway interrupted. "I think Dolittle's . . . the most remarkable surgeon I've ever seen."

"Righto," Weller said. "He's here to *stay*! He's the top dog around here, ha ha." Weller laughed. "I think we're ready to sign."

Calloway turned and entered the operating room with Weller.

"Incredible work, Doctors," Calloway said.

"Bravo!" Weller added. "Really inspiring stuff!"

"Welcome aboard. I feel like I just bought myself a winning franchise," Calloway said.

"Sorry, but you didn't buy anything." Dolittle smiled. "We're not for sale!"

"Yeah!" Reiss smiled in agreement. Weller turned, glaring at Calloway. "Who needs those wackos, anyway?" Weller said. "We can do it without 'em—" He was cut off by pigeon droppings, which hit him squarely on the head as the birds flew in through the open window. Weller looked up, his mouth open—a big mistake as the pigeon hit its target.

Calloway started laughing at Weller's misfortune. In the next second, the pigeons decorated his head too.

The pigeons laughed and high-fived each other with their tails. "Bull's-eye," the female called.

"Let's go find their cars!" the male suggested, and they flew out the window.

13

The next day the Dolittle family was home, recovering from all the excitement. The tiger returned to the circus and rested in his cage under the watchful eyes of his friends. Maya was doing her homework in her room, where the still unhatched egg sat on a soft towel.

Rodney was munching on party mix when he suddenly looked up. "Hey, hey, hey!" he shouted. "We got a birth here," he said as the huge egg began to hatch.

The shell opened slowly, and a baby alligator popped out and stared right into the guinea pig's eyes.

"Mama," the alligator said.

"Not me, Slick!" Rodney said.

"Mama," the alligator said.

"You see scales on me?" Rodney argued. "I'm all

118

fur. You look like those dudes on tennis shirts." Rodney laughed. Lucky looked over and started barking. Maya looked up from her books.

"My egg!" she yelled. "Mom! Dad! My swan's egg's hatching. My swan—my swan's a—a *lizard*?" she said in surprise as everyone came running in.

"What the heck is that, Doc?" Lucky asked.

"That would be a baby alligator! Maya's new pet alligator." Dolittle smiled.

"Oh! Cool!" Maya cried. She picked up the small, scaly baby.

"Bring him to the new office tomorrow so we can check him out, okay, honey?" Dolittle said.

"Thanks, Dad."

The next day Maya carried her little alligator in a decorated shoe box to her dad's new office. She walked into the waiting room, where there was a line of humans and animals leading into Dolittle's office. The sign on the door read DOCTOR DOLITTLE— ANIMALS AND PEOPLE WELCOME! The logo showed a human hand holding an animal's paw.

Maya went up to the receptionist.

"Hi, Maya," Diane said.

"I'm here to see my dad for an appointment, for my new pet," Maya said. She opened her shoe box. "Look at my baby alligator! Isn't he the cutest thing?"

Epilogue

Lucky leaned back, smiling, as he finished the story he had started telling two hours before. "And that's the story of the tiger, Dr. Dolittle, and me," he said.

"Talk about a shaggy dog story!" Spike the schnauzer said, laughing.

"I know how to tell when you're lying," Rocky the retriever said. "Your mouth moves." The dogs all laughed at Lucky.

"I'm telling you, it's all true. Every last word," Lucky said.

"If it's all true, then what are you doing out here with us?" asked Spike.

"Hey, I'm still one of the guys, aren't I? I like to hang out, run with the pack every so often," Lucky said.

Just then John Dolittle walked over. "Lucky?" he called. "What are you doing out here?"

"Nothing," Lucky said. He ran up to meet Dolittle. "Just hangin' with the boys."

Dolittle nodded. "Okay, that's cool, but come on, we have rounds to make."

The other dogs all stood up, stunned as Lucky walked off with Dolittle. Lucky turned to give them a look.

"See you, fellas," Dolittle called over his shoulder.

Dolittle and Lucky walked up the street. Dolittle talked and gestured to Lucky. People who passed them and hadn't heard about the now famous doctor who could speak to animals stopped and watched in amazement.

Lucky and Dr. Dolittle didn't care if people stared. They were having a fine conversation and didn't even notice.